Hidden Away

By

Elizabeth Castle

Name: Castle, Elizabeth, author

Title: Unraveled

Description: Series: The Cantwell Quartet

Publisher: In The Air Publishing

Identifiers: ISBN 9781967731244 (ebook) | ISBN 9781967731251 (paperback) | ISBN 9798305404180 (amazon hardcover)

Cover Design by betibup33

Chapter One

Dr. Isaac Brandt was not having a good day. It had started when he knocked his coffee over and the porcelain cup splintered and spilled everywhere. Then he had somehow managed to kick his big toe into the stool at his kitchen counter. While cursing and trying to clean up the mess, he had cracked his head on the overhang of the island counter.

Then because days that start like that continue like that, his laptop died and wouldn't restart, he accidentally bleached his favorite pair of jeans, and burned his dinner. So it was with the house smelling like smoke, the kitchen floor still sticky from the coffee, his laptop in pieces at his kitchen table, and wearing bleached jeans that he opened the door when it rang.

"You look like hell." Nash Camhion came in, and he glanced toward the kitchen. His black brow rose.

"Don't ask." Isaac shut the door behind his friend. He knew how he looked. His hair was disheveled, his glasses were askew, and his usually impeccable appearance was marred by the untucked shirt and bleach-stained pants.

"Have to. Did you burn something?"

"Dinner."

Nash headed toward the kitchen, staring at the burnt mess. "May I ask when the last time you burned a meal was?"

Isaac shrugged as he scraped the rest of the burnt food

into the trash and set the pan to soak. "I don't know. Six, maybe."

Nash took a seat at the island while Isaac set about making a replacement meal. Nash watched as Isaac deftly chopped a pile of vegetables. "I would have loved to see the look on your dad's face the first time he caught you hanging out with the cook."

Isaac set a pot to boil. He and his father had been at odds for as long as Isaac could remember. Dr. Theodore Brandt looked down on everyone, and that included his wife and son. Isaac had learned at an early age what type of man his father was. And he knew even as a child that he didn't want to be anything like him. Instead of studying and reading, in his youth Isaac had spent most of his free time with the cook, the gardener, or one of the ladies who came in to clean. It hadn't been by design to anger his father that Isaac had come to enjoy cooking, gardening, and cleaning more than he did studying, but by the time Isaac was old enough to want to defy his father, he'd already succeeded by excelling in tasks his father thought beneath him. His father had been horrified. His father had called him a plebeian, a commoner, ordinary, and every other word he could think of in his anger to put him down.

Isaac didn't spend much time thinking about his father, but Nash's comment did make him smile. "Horrified is a mild word."

Nash accepted the beer Isaac handed him and pointed it at the disassembled laptop. "So, get any work done today? You said you'd have the first book ready."

Isaac rubbed his forehead where a headache was

forming. "Laptop crashed. Won't restart. I was trying to figure out why it wouldn't turn on. I have the first draft done, but unless you want to read it on your phone, I can't show you."

"Did you order another one?"

Isaac just looked at him.

Nash held up a hand. "Right. No laptop. You know, you could get with the times and get a smart phone. It's embarrassing when you pull that old flip phone out of your pocket."

Isaac laughed. He'd heard it before, but Isaac didn't have a love for technology. His laptop made writing easier, but he still took notes by hand, graded papers by hand, read a physical book, and preferred to indulge in a game of chess or do a crossword puzzle rather than gaming on his laptop. His students at Georgetown called him a relic behind his back. But that didn't bother him. Eventually even his most tech-savvy students came to appreciate his teaching methods, and he liked to think he was keeping the traditions of books and literature alive one student at a time.

Isaac turned to protest when he heard Nash on the phone.

"Hi, Lilah. Tomorrow, I need you to get Isaac a new laptop. You can take it out of the company's expense account. And could you have it delivered to his house? Yeah, his died, and if we don't get him a new one, he's liable to start handwriting his new book. Thanks. See you tomorrow."

"Why did you do that?" Isaac began sautéing the fresh

pile of vegetables he had cut up.

"You have the worst handwriting. And Lilah is a woman of many talents. She'll get you fixed up with the perfect laptop."

Isaac pointed at him with the spatula. "You know how to order a computer as well as she does. And you know exactly what to buy. I wish you would stop."

Nash was all innocence. "Stop what? You agreed to let Lilah work on the art for the graphic novels to complement the game. That means you need a laptop."

Isaac went back to assembling dinner. Isaac and Nash, along with two other friends, Gideon and Trenton, had started a company called Cantwell. Cantwell's first project was a video game based on a novel Isaac had written two summers ago. Nash had taken the idea and fast-tracked a role-playing adventure game based on the characters and story in Isaac's book. Fantasy and romance were a departure for Isaac; he preferred science fiction when he tackled fiction, but the book had come to him, and he had written it during a two-week binge during summer break.

The story featured four men, four brothers, though not by blood. At its core, the book was about the four of them. They called themselves the quartet, and they had been friends since junior high. Each of the four men in the book described one of them: their looks, their personalities, their loves, and their fears. And while Isaac didn't see them as knights in shining armor, the tale of four men fighting for the women who haunted their dreams was somewhat autobiographical.

Nash was the leader, both in life and in the book. In the

book, the dark-haired prince is seeking revenge for the murder of his father, then his fiancée. He starts the quest to find the man responsible. In real life, Nash lost his grandfather, who had been murdered by the man who had kidnapped Nash. Years later, he lost his fiancée to drugs. Grief had drawn them together, but Maggie's grief had been more than she could bear.

Gideon was the oldest, though not by more than two months, and very much the protector. Gideon thought of himself more as a sword than a shield, but Isaac saw both in him in equal parts. The character in his book bore the scars that Gideon bore and was the first into battle. On the surface, Gideon was a cop. The sword, as Isaac saw it. He sought to enforce laws and hunt down those who broke them. But inside there was insecurity and a reservedness. In that, Isaac saw him as a protector, a shield. Often his first instinct was to protect those smaller and weaker than him. It was almost a year now since Gideon married Penny, Nash's younger sister. He would protect Penny with his life. And he wouldn't hesitate to put himself between himself and any danger to those he loved, including the quartet. As a child, Gideon had saved Nash from the hands of his kidnapper.

Trenton was the youngest, and as Gideon was wont to point out, the shortest. Trenton was the comedian of the group, but beneath the humor was a very serious soul. These past months had done much to alleviate the shadows of the past that he had lived with his whole life. And his wife, Ginny, had brought a new spark to the humor. And Ginny's daughter, Gwenny, had brought out a new level of love and protectiveness. There was lightness in him now, a true embrace of happiness and love.

Isaac, well, he thought of himself as the glue. If their life were a book, Nash was the book cover. The one that would draw you in. Gideon was the book spine, the one that kept the book standing. Trenton was the pages, with the words that enticed the reader to turn the page. And Isaac was the glue; the one that held the pieces together.

Gideon said he was the voice of reason. Nash said he was the professor. Trenton called him a stick in the mud. And he was. Isaac was studious like his father. When he'd gotten older, despite not wanting to love anything his father loved, he'd learned to love to read. Not the boring dissertations that his father read, but stories of space and time, stories of survival and discovery, and stories of the heart and strength that lived inside of people. Isaac loved history; he loved literature. That was what he taught. He loved language and found a whole new world by reading, in their original language, books from around the world.

But what Isaac really loved to do was write and cook. There was something satisfying in the creation of both a book and a perfect meal. And when Nash had asked him when the last time he'd burned a meal was, six was probably accurate. He'd started hanging out with the cook at five, and when he'd turned six, the cook had finally given in and let him help. The cook had called him an old soul. Young Isaac had been delighted with the description and could only agree.

Isaac took the meal off the burner and set it to cool. "Why don't you clean up the mess I made with the laptop, and we can eat?"

Nash picked it all up and tossed it in the trash. "Done."

Isaac glared at him. "We recycle electronics in this house."

Nash left it in the trash. "Feel free to dig it out. I'm sure Lilah would be happy to recycle it for you."

Lust and guilt punched him in the gut. He'd gotten used to the lust part. He'd known her for well over a year now. Nash had hired her to help develop and direct the graphic art for Cantwell. She was an incredibly gifted artist. She called herself an illustrator, but it was more than that. She'd helped bring Cantwell to life. He was as attracted to her mind as he was her body. She had long red hair that fell in waves to her waist. The freckles that were liberally sprinkled across her nose and cheeks enhanced her natural beauty. But her violet eyes were what drew him in. Lavender eyes, he thought.

She only hit his shoulder in height, and her clothes got baggier by the day. Lately he'd seen dark circles under her eyes. That's where the guilt came in. In the six months since he'd been attacked, she'd run his errands, picked up his dry cleaning, ordered his groceries, and when his sight was at its worst, she'd helped him type up his work and even helped him pay his bills online. The past month, the vision in his left eye was good enough for him to handle the brightness of his laptop. And the tinted glasses he now wore every day also helped.

Isaac finished preparing the meal and brought two overflowing plates to the table.

Nash picked up his fork and dug in. "I don't know how

you make everything taste so good. And I still have never met anyone besides you who makes their own noodles by hand."

Isaac didn't answer. Homemade noodles were Nash's favorite. Isaac refused to use electric mixers or devices to make his noodles. "Does Delilah seem okay to you?"

Nash's arm stopped midway to his mouth. "No. I don't think she is, if you want the truth. Between your ammonia burns and her being held at gunpoint by a madwoman, I don't think either of you are doing well."

Isaac didn't want to talk about his burns. The attack had been meant for Trenton. The man who threw the concentrated liquid ammonia at his face had been hiding in the bushes. It was luck and timing that Isaac had even seen the man. And when Isaac saw the man coming at his best friend, Isaac had acted on instinct and put himself between Trenton and the attacker. The only thing Isaac remembered about the attack was the excruciating pain. His right eye was permanently damaged, and the doctors had told him there was nothing else they could do. His left eye had healed, but it had taken time and two surgeries. He had seen a plastic surgeon who said he could help reduce the scarring, but Isaac didn't see the point. If his vision couldn't be restored, what did a few burn scars matter?

Nash leaned over and put a hand on top of Isaac's. "Trenton still blames himself. Ginny does, too. More Ginny. I know you don't blame them. But I know how being a victim feels, Isaac. And if you won't talk to professionals, then you should at least talk to your friends."

Isaac had heard the same argument from his doctors.

They said he'd experienced a trauma and that he needed to process it. "I know Trenton and Ginny feel guilty. No matter how many times I tell them I don't blame them and that it wasn't their fault. I can't talk to Trenton about what happened."

Nash squeezed his hand. "You two were always the closest of the quartet. But I've got a good ear, you know."

Isaac closed his eyes. "I know you do. But you have your own demons to deal with."

Nash released him. "Yeah, but my demons are twenty-six years old. Yours are new. And I didn't lose my vision. You've been on leave from teaching for almost six months. You barely leave this house except for doctor's appointments. It took you four months to write the first draft of our graphic novel. Something that I know you could have knocked out in a month before this happened. What happened will never leave you. Lilah, too. But she's seeing a therapist that Gideon put her in touch with, and she's trying to process what happened. Don't let what happened to me be the reason you keep it to yourself."

Isaac swallowed the lump in his throat. "I know. But I'm not sure what there is to say. It all happened so fast. And I barely remember anything after the initial attack and my waking up in the hospital. All I can think is that if the ammonia had hit Trenton straight in the face, we would have buried our friend. I guess for now, that's enough for me."

Nash nodded. "And me. I always thought Gideon was the one we had to worry about. The next pact we make, I think it needs to be no more crazies. Between my cousin

Clara kidnapping Penny and trying to kill her, a crazed cultist trying to kill Trenton, and the crazed cultist's mother trying to kill Lilah, Ginny, and her daughter Gwenny, I think we can all agree."

Isaac laughed, even though Nash was dead serious. "I think we can all agree on that."

They resumed eating. When Nash finished his plate, he sat back in his chair. "Man, that's good stuff. I'm telling you; you're wasted in academia. Next Cantwell venture is a restaurant, and I'm putting you in the kitchen."

Isaac finished off his beer. "Somehow I can't picture Gideon in a waiter's uniform."

Nash laughed. "How about Trenton as the busboy?"

Isaac smiled. "Works for me. And I assume you're the maître d'."

Nash undid his belt. "Yep. I'm the one who will charm them inside."

Isaac went and grabbed another couple of beers. "Cheers."

Nash tapped his bottle to Isaac's. "So speaking of charm, Lilah and I have a date on Saturday."

Isaac choked on his beer. "You what?"

Nash smiled behind his beer. "A date. You keep saying you're not interested in her. And Lilah and I spend a lot of time together. She invited me to dinner. I accepted."

Isaac slammed the bottle onto the table. "She asked you out?"

Nash took a large swallow. "Yep. Figured why not. She's a little young for my taste, but she's cute, she's smart, and when we're not arguing about the game, she's fun to hang out with. You don't mind, do you?"

Isaac's eyes narrowed over the beer bottle. "Mind? Why would I mind?"

Nash sat back in his chair. "Good."

It took everything in him to clean up the mess, talk shop, and not punch the smile off Nash's face. By the time he shut and locked his front door, his teeth ached from clenching his jaw.

Isaac passed a mirror on the way to the stairs. He wanted to punch his reflection. Delilah could date anyone she wanted. He wasn't anything to her. She barely tolerated his presence. When they worked together, she barely said a word that wasn't related to work. Even when she was in his home, she kept her distance, kept all chatter strictly professional, and said her goodbyes.

And so what if she liked Nash? Nash wasn't as much of a playboy as the press painted him to be, not these days anyway. Being the heir to the Camhion fortune garnered him a lot of attention. Right now he was using that attention to his advantage. Word was already buzzing around Cantwell and the upcoming release of the beta version of the game. And women were always flocking to him. He had model good looks, a muscular and fit body, with black hair and smoldering gray eyes. Because he rarely went out with a woman more than a couple of times, his affairs were few and far between. The playboy persona helped keep people from seeing more than he wanted them to see. Why would Delilah be immune?

But damn it, why Delilah? He'd been trying to figure out a way to get into her good graces. But that was before the attack. He hadn't come up with a good idea then. And now it seemed impossible. He might not be disabled, but now that he suffered from headaches and was physically scarred, he couldn't burden her with that. She had enough to deal with when it came to her mother and her mother's illness; he'd be nothing but a burden to her. He was also a reminder of the attack she'd suffered. These days she barely looked at him. And it made seeing her, wanting her, that much more difficult for him.

He supposed it was inevitable she'd show up the next morning. Her hair was covered in an orange knit cap, and under her open purple coat was a pair of denim overalls he found sexy on her and a bright green and yellow striped flannel shirt. She had a new laptop in her arms. Groggy from another late night, he answered his door with a growl. "What are you doing here?"

Lilah held up the box. "Laptop. Nash sent me."

Isaac stepped back so she could come in. His heart ached watching her, her violet eyes wide with surprise at his tone. "He said to have one delivered."

Lilah stopped halfway on her way to the staircase. "And what do you call this? I'm delivering it."

Isaac tried to grab it, but she turned and quickly climbed the stairs.

Lilah's back was to him when he came into the office. There were days when he would swear her smell lingered in the air after she was gone. It made getting work done difficult.

Lilah grabbed a pair of scissors and cut the tape on the box. She started to unbox it when Isaac reached over and took the box from her. "Thank you for delivering it."

Lilah's brows knitted as he walked to the office door and gestured for her to go.

She crossed her arms over her chest, her red hair swirling around her shoulders as she shook her head at him. "Are you okay?"

Isaac felt his temper fray. "I'm not an invalid, Delilah. I don't need your help."

Lilah's mouth opened; her lavender eyes narrowed. "Excuse me?"

Isaac, now angry as her beautiful face frowned at him, came and took her arm. "I can do this myself. I don't need or want you here."

Before she could protest, he led her down the stairs, pushed her outside, closed the door, and locked it behind him.

Lilah knocked a few times and called his name. But Isaac just leaned against the door, eyes closed. He didn't relax until he heard her car pull out of his driveway. Cursing her and Nash, he took the laptop upstairs, where it took him the rest of the day to set it up. No doubt Delilah would have had it done in no time.

But after the way he behaved, he doubted she'd be back.

Chapter Two

Lilah sipped her sparkling water, looking around the restaurant and anxiously waiting for her mother and her date.

Nash handed her his glass of scotch. "Want a sip? Might calm your nerves."

Lilah shook her head. "I shouldn't have agreed to this."

Nash was calm and the voice of reason. "Which part? The part where your mother, a grown woman, is having her boyfriend pick her up for a date? Or the part where you agreed to have dinner with them so that you could meet him? Or the part where you asked me to come with you so you wouldn't have to meet him alone?"

Lilah took the glass from his hand and took a sip. "You forgot the other part. The part where I asked you to come with me so that my mother would think I have a date of my own."

Nash patted her back as she coughed on the potent liquor. He slipped the glass from her hand. "Ah, yes. The date decoy. I think that's my favorite. How adoring am I supposed to be?"

Lilah gave him a dirty look. "What?"

Nash leaned over and set his lips lightly on hers. "You know, adoring."

Lilah laughed against his lips. "I don't think my mother is into public displays of affection. You can hold my hand."

Nash raised his head. "How boring. I'd rather kiss you."

Lilah hummed. "I have a feeling you've kissed a lot of girls over the years. But I don't think you really meant them."

Nash leaned back. "The kisses? I did once. Seems a long time ago."

Lilah was sorry she'd said that. "I'm sorry, Nash. That wasn't very nice of me."

Nash took her hand and toyed with her fingers. "I've come to the conclusion that there is not a mean bone in your body. So when are you going to give Isaac a chance?"

Lilah didn't pretend she didn't understand, though it was tempting. Nash had been matchmaking since the first day she'd met the quartet. "He threw me out. I think that says it all."

She'd told Nash what had happened when she'd dropped off the laptop. Lilah hadn't been sure what to do. She'd never seen him angry. His good eye was a blue heated laser as he'd watched her. He always seemed, well, steady, she supposed. Even keel, like nothing phased him. Between working on the side quests of the game together and her taking care of some of the things he couldn't while his eyes healed, she'd spent a lot of time alone with him recently. He never seemed frustrated or angry, or mad or disgusted. And given what he'd gone through, he'd have every right to feel those things. But he seemed to take everything in stride. She knew he was doing a sight better than she was. He'd had concentrated ammonia tossed in his face. He lost vision in one eye and damage to the other. He bore visible scars. She couldn't sleep because a woman who ultimately didn't hurt her had pointed a gun at her. In the scale of things, what he went through was much worse.

The scars bothered her, though not for the reason one might think. When she'd first met him, and she'd started the art for the game, she'd taken his likeness and she'd toughened up his looks and added scars to his face. The fact that he now had scars, not unlike the ones she'd drawn, bothered her. A lot. It was like she'd somehow seen into the future, or somehow willed something bad to happen. On top of that, the only reason he'd been outside was because Trenton was outside after he'd walked her to her car. As illogical as it was, it left her feeling somehow to blame.

"Where are you at, Lilah?" Nash turned her chin toward him.

"What? Oh, sorry. I drifted."

Nash held her chin. "It wasn't a good place. You do that a lot, you know."

Lilah glanced at the front door again. "I know. They're late."

Nash released her and leaned back. "Not anymore."

Lilah's mother was being pushed in a wheelchair by a medium-height man with gray, thinning hair and a paunch. Lilah rose. "I was getting worried."

Priscilla Fitzpatrick raised her cheek as her daughter bent to kiss it. "You know me; I take forever to get where I'm going. I want you to meet Robert. He's a retired doctor at MedStar Washington Hospital Center. I met him while we were both having some tests. This is my daughter, Delilah."

Robert held out his hand. "You can call me Rob."

Lilah shook his hand. "You can call me Lilah. It's nice to finally meet you. I didn't even know about you until last week."

Rob pushed Priscilla's chair up to the table and then held Lilah's chair for her. "Your mother said she hadn't told you about us. To be honest, we've talked more on the phone than in person. But I wanted to meet you. She talks about you all the time."

Priscilla was looking at Nash. "And this young man?"

Lilah blushed. "Mom, this is Nash Camhion."

Nash held out his hand to Priscilla. "It's nice to meet you, Mrs. Fitzpatrick. I'm an admirer of your daughter."

Nash then held a hand out to Rob. "Nice to meet you as well."

Rob took a seat. "Camhion? Not as in Eldridge Camhion?"

Nash nodded. "My father."

Rob grinned. "Well, I'll be. I met your father, though I can't say I know him well. He's a big donor at the hospital. Built a wing, I believe."

Priscilla was looking at him, then her daughter. "He's not the one."

Lilah's eyes pleaded with Nash, then turned to her mother. "I don't know what you mean."

Priscilla folded her arms across her chest. "I may be sick, but my brain still works. He's your boss, not your boyfriend. He's not the one."

Nash couldn't stop grinning as he took a sip of his scotch. "As to that, I know who is. And I am an admirer of your daughter. But of her talent. I consider her a friend.

And I did want to meet you."

Priscilla nodded in approval. "So who is the one?"

Nash tipped his head. "Did you see the drawings Lilah did of us?"

"Mmm. I did. The Cantwell Quartet, I believe she calls you."

"The tall blond with the military-cut hair and the scars on his face."

Priscilla approved. "Yes, the intelligent one. Not that you aren't, dear. But I hear he's a professor at Georgetown. And he writes books on history. Believe he dabbles in science fiction."

Rob's jaw dropped. "You don't mean Dr. Isaac Brandt, do you? The man is brilliant. And he more than dabbles in science fiction. He's a master. I hear he's departed into fantasy, and his new book is based on a video game."

Nash signaled the waiter. "Yes, but it's the other way around. The game is based on his book. He and Lilah are now working on a graphic novel series based on the game."

Rob shook his head. "I can't wait to read them."

Dinner was going well, and the four of them had a nice time. Lilah was still a bit in shock. Rob wasn't quite what she had imagined. And her mother was blushing like a schoolgirl. There were times like these when, if it weren't for the wheelchair, she wouldn't know her mother was sick.

They were having dessert when her mother revealed the real purpose of the dinner.

"Rob and I have been talking, and we're going to take a trip."

Lilah dropped her fork. "You're what?"

Rob took Priscilla's hand. "A trip. We were talking and she's never been to Maine. It's too cold now to see whales, or do the summer stuff, but a friend of mine owns a lovely bed and breakfast. There is a downstairs bedroom that would be perfect for Priscilla. And the bathroom is fully accessible for her with a walk-in shower. It's perfect."

Maine in the dead of winter didn't sound like fun to her; Lilah would go for her mother, but she just couldn't. "Mom, I can't go to Maine. Isaac and I have just started on the artwork for his novel."

Her mother was still smiling, but her tone changed. "You're not invited, dear."

Lilah's mouth dropped. "But who is going to take care of you?"

Rob cleared his throat. "I am."

Nash took Lilah's arm and tugged her against him so that their shoulders touched. "Sounds romantic. Too bad I can't get Lilah to go away with me."

Priscilla wagged a finger at him. "You are a charmer; I'll give you that. And if you were the one, I'd gladly let you two run off together. But you're not."

Lilah leaned against Nash, absorbing his strong presence beside her. Then she looked at Rob. "What kind of doctor were you?"

Rob's tone was serious. "I was a general practitioner for a few years before specializing in cardiology. Your mom is in good hands; I promise."

Lilah was a bit shell-shocked, but the rest of dinner went well. Her mother was getting tired, so Rob paid the bill and wished them good night before wheeling her mother out to the car. When she said don't wait up for her, Lilah had numbly nodded her head.

Nash helped her to her feet. "You look lost for words. Your mom never had a boyfriend before?"

Lilah dropped her hands to her sides, a bit flustered. "No. No boyfriends. It wasn't long after my dad died that we learned of her diagnosis. For a few years, signs of the disease weren't there. But then it became difficult to walk. Her legs wouldn't do what she wanted them to do."

Nash helped her into her coat and led them outside. Nash rarely drove, but he'd done so tonight. "Freaking you out a little bit, thinking about your mother having sex?"

Lilah's voice was a squeak. "What?"

Nash laughed; he couldn't help it. "Jeez, Lilah. Your mom is a grown woman. And she's going home with her boyfriend. What do you think they're doing? Playing cards?"

Lilah blew warm air on her hands as they walked to where Nash had parked. "They could be playing cards."

Nash put his arm around her waist. "And the hotel in Maine? Just a trip between buddies?"

Lilah let out a puff of air. "Okay, so they're probably having sex. I should be happy for her. In a couple of years, a trip like that will likely be impossible. And between my dad and me, she was always taking care of one of us."

Nash squeezed her to his side. "And now you take care of her. But maybe it's okay to let Rob take care of her, too. He seems nice. A jolly sort of fellow. He tells a great story. I see why your mom likes him."

Lilah looked down at her feet. The sensible, rubber-soled flats were practical but not stylish. "It seemed like things were always going the wrong way in our family. I never told you why I limp."

Nash navigated them around a patch of ice. "No, you haven't. Injury?"

Lilah sighed and kept walking. "Problem at birth. Took years to fix. And then fix what the doctor did wrong. Let's just say my medical bills were more than my parents could handle. Things were better when I went to college, but then I had college to pay for. And when my dad died six years ago, things got bad again. I knew something was wrong, but my mom kept denying it. I finally made Mom go to the doctor. I hadn't realized she wasn't well until long after my dad passed. The doctor diagnosed her with multiple sclerosis. She'd been ignoring the symptoms for years. Because of me."

They reached the car, and Nash opened the door. "Because of your bills?"

Lilah knew that Nash and his family had money. Lots of it. But he seemed to sympathize and understand that for most, money wasn't in abundance. "She didn't have insurance after my dad died. And it took years to pay off my bills, and that was with insurance. So she wasn't willing to have tests done that she couldn't afford to pay. So I made her go and I paid for them. Or at least I'm trying to. This really is the best job I've ever had. You four overpay me, and Trenton has been a godsend."

Nash helped her into the car. "You're worth every cent. But yes, Trenton is a wizard with money, that's for sure. He likes investing. And you were the reason he finally opened his own firm."

Trenton had said much the same to her. That she'd shown him other ways to help people. He helped them invest and taught them what they needed to know to keep moving forward toward their financial goals. He was keeping her afloat.

Nash drove her home. "I've been thinking. With your mother out of town for two weeks, it's a great opportunity for you to meet with Isaac's agent. I was going to take Isaac to Vermont to meet with him. Isaac loves to ski. I thought it would be good for him to go outside and get some fresh air. Isaac is fighting me, of course, but he finally agreed to go, though he did say that he wasn't going to ski. Do you ski?"

Lilah wasn't following. "No. But what does my mom's trip have to do with you and Isaac going to Vermont?"

Nash's face was in the shadows. "Well, I have a conflict. And after Isaac's outburst this week, I'm even more convinced he needs to get out. And I already booked two hotel rooms at a nearby ski resort. We were going to meet up there and talk business. I want you to take him."

* * *

Lilah stood on the front steps of Isaac's house and rang the bell. She loved the house. The siding was yellow, and the shutters were white. The roof was a soft blue-gray. In the spring, there would be flowers in the planters on each side of the front door. The house had gingerbread trim beneath the peaks of the roof line. It wasn't flashy like

Trenton's house. It wasn't elegant like Penny and Gideon's or Nash's. This house had an old fashion charm. Unlike its owner, who was now glaring at her.

Isaac let her in. "I thought we were going to meet at the office when I got back. Trenton's already here helping me pack for the trip. Apparently, he thinks I need help. Like someone else I know."

A masculine voice called from upstairs. "Lilah, is that you? You're right on time."

Lilah ignored Isaac. If he was grumpy now, wait until he found out she was the one driving him. She didn't want to contemplate being cooped up in a car with him for that long. It was almost an eight-hour drive, and that was without stopping. Nash had said Isaac adamantly refused to fly. So she got to be the chauffeur.

Trenton came down with a large suitcase and a duffel bag. "I packed a cooler in the kitchen. Isaac, why don't you go get it?"

Trenton came and kissed Lilah on the cheek. "You're a saint. Nash has an investor meeting that came up, and it's a golden opportunity not to be missed. And Ginny and Gwenny are getting over a cold, so I've been playing nurse. Gideon has to work."

Lilah's gaze went to the kitchen. "He's really mad at me."

Trenton had noticed. "Not just you. He's been a bear the past few days. I was going to sick Penny on him, but she's not feeling well, either. I think she caught Gwenny's cold."

Lilah's gaze softened when she thought of the little girl. She was seven and full of sass. She loved seeing Trenton with the little girl. She knew he'd been nervous about becoming Gwenny's dad, but Gwenny had embraced him. Ginny wasn't Gwenny's biological mother, so for Gwenny, a stepdad was just the same as getting a real dad.

"You'd think we were going to be gone for a month. This thing is packed to the brim." Isaac came in carrying a huge and obviously heavy cooler.

Trenton winked at Lilah. "Lots of unhealthy food in there. Have a safe trip. I'm going to get out of here so you can leave. It's a long drive."

Isaac turned on Lilah. "What does he mean?"

Lilah lifted the duffle bag and almost fell over. "What did he pack in here?"

Isaac yanked the bag from her grip. "Well?"

Lilah grabbed the handle of his suitcase. It was heavier, but at least it had wheels. She headed for the door. "Nash asked me to drive. He can't make it, and he says I should meet your agent. I get credit for the artwork, so my name will be on the graphic novels. Your agent has agreed to represent me as part of the package deal for the books. Anyway, Nash said your fiction publisher is interested in the project and that your agent wants to size me up, so to speak. Mostly to make sure I can deliver the same caliber of work you do. I've brought my work portfolio to show him. But it is a long drive, so we should go."

Lilah managed to get outside and was trying to figure out how she was going to lift the suitcase to carry it down the stairs.

Isaac closed and locked the house. Then he grabbed the suitcase like it weighed nothing and hauled it down the stairs. "Nash has gone too far this time."

Lilah had to jog to catch up. "What do you mean?"

"Don't tell me you haven't noticed. He's been trying to throw the two of us together for over a year. First it was the portraits. Then it was the collaboration on the game, then the side quests. Now it's the graphic novels. We could have hired anyone to do them, but he wanted you."

Lilah stopped in her tracks. "And you didn't?"

Isaac opened the hatch of his SUV. "He thinks he can manufacture a romance."

Lilah felt tears clogging her throat. "Manufacture a romance. So Nash only wants me to do the art for the books so that we'll spend time together?"

Isaac went to her car and pulled out the suitcase she had stashed in her back seat. "Yes. Hell, he knows a few graphic novelists. It's how he got the idea. But his plan won't work."

Lilah's eyes stung, and she willed herself not to cry. It was too late to back out. She'd signed a contract with Cantwell to do the art. But maybe if the agent didn't like her, she could get out of it. She thought the team wanted her to do the books. She had doubts, too, about her drawing. She was more confident in her computer work than in her hand drawing. But the graphic novels had seemed like a great opportunity, maybe even a new direction for her career. She'd always wanted to write; she had lots of ideas, and doing art for a graphic novel had excited her. Now she felt sick to her stomach.

She was quiet as he tossed her much lighter bag into the back of the SUV. She put on her sunglasses to cover her wet eyes and set the navigation to the address Nash had given her and buckled her seat belt. She glanced at Isaac. His jaw was clenched. She put the car in reverse and prayed for the trip to be over quickly.

Chapter Three

He was being an ass. He knew it. But he'd been in a bad mood from the moment Nash had told him he was taking Delilah on a date. Damn it, she was his. Not Nash's. It hadn't gotten past Isaac's notice that Nash had gotten exactly what he wanted by making him jealous. Nash wanted to force him to acknowledge that he had feelings for Delilah. But what scorched him was that Delilah had asked Nash out. Not the other way around. She had initiated the date. And yes, jealousy tore at him. Nash always had a way with the ladies. And it was clear that Delilah preferred Nash.

It was all Gideon's fault. Him and his dream and the drawings of the women. Delilah had done the drawings of the men. She'd used photographs Trenton had taken and made the quartet into the game's heroes. Delilah was going to draw the women, but when she saw what Gideon had drawn, she'd refused. Gideon had drawn four women, one for each hero. The women in the game were trapped and came to the heroes in dreams. Just as Isaac had written it.

When Gideon and Penny hooked up, it had been a relief to everyone. Those two had tap danced around each other long enough. But Penny was convinced she was the woman in the first painting that Gideon drew from his dreams. And that woman was the heroine for Gideon's character. Then Trenton had been convinced Ginny was the woman in his drawing. No one in the group had been happy about that.

Ginny had come to find Trenton and had brought trouble with her. It hadn't been intentional, but had she never come, Isaac wouldn't have been hurt, and Delilah wouldn't have had a gun pointed at her. But then again, Trenton wouldn't be happy; he wouldn't have Ginny, and he wouldn't have Gwenny.

The redhead was for Isaac's character, or so everyone thought. At first, Isaac laughed it off. But the woman in the drawing looked so much like Delilah. He would know; he'd made a study of her. And from behind, with her red hair flowing down her back, Delilah looked just like the woman in the painting. The only thing missing was the white dress the woman wore. All he'd ever seen Delilah in were overalls and t-shirts, or baggy jeans and flannels.

Three hours into the drive, Lilah pulled into a gas station. Without saying a word, she handed him the keys and left the SUV. Isaac figured that was his cue to fill it up. Glasses on, he filled the tank. He saw a little girl with her dad pointing at him. He was rarely out these days, and it took a minute to realize she was pointing at him and his scars. He put a smile on his face and waved at her. The girl tucked her head against her father's leg but tentatively waved back.

"Well, at least you didn't scowl at her the way you do me."

Isaac followed Lilah to the back of the SUV, where she dug two cans of iced tea from the cooler. She opened one and handed it to Isaac. She then opened the other one and took a large swallow.

"I wasn't scowling at you."

Lilah shrugged. "Are you hungry? Trenton packed enough junk food in here to last a week."

"I'm not hungry. And I wouldn't scowl at a little girl."

Lilah pulled out a Snickers for herself. "Just big girls then. You should hit the bathroom before we go. We've got another five hours to go."

He headed off to the men's room. He then took a moment to get a grip. So what if Delilah went out with Nash? It didn't mean anything. Then it occurred to him that Delilah shouldn't be on this trip. She should be at home with her mom.

Isaac washed his hands and left. He found Lilah leaning against the car. "Want to call a truce?"

Lilah tipped her sunglasses down to get a better look at him. "Did you hit your head or something in the bathroom?"

Isaac held up a hand. "You're not all sweetness and light, either. You've not liked me since the day we met."

Lilah pushed her sunglasses back up to hide her eyes. "Who says I don't like you?"

Isaac went around, got into the SUV, and slammed the door.

Lilah climbed in. "Well?"

Isaac took a deep breath. "Just drive. It was stupid to think we could call a truce. I'm pissed, and you're the most unfriendly woman I know. At least with me. With Nash, you're all smiles and laughs."

Lilah started the engine. "Do you pay any attention at work? Nash and I fight like cats and dogs."

"Then why did you ask him out on a date?"

Lilah turned in her seat. "How did you know that?"

Isaac gritted his teeth. "Nash told me. Said you asked him out to dinner."

Lilah bared her teeth. "I did. And look where it got me? Stuck in a car with you."

Isaac wasn't sure what to say to that. Apparently, she said enough because she pulled out of the gas station and got back on the highway.

Isaac tried a different approach. "Who is staying with your mother?"

"What, Nash didn't tell you?"

Isaac just watched her until she squirmed in her seat.

"She's with Rob. He's her new boyfriend. Mom says she's feeling well enough to take a trip. So they're in Maine right now doing who knows what at a bed and breakfast near the ocean."

Isaac frowned. "So the only free time you have to yourself, Nash sends you to babysit me?"

Lilah shifted uncomfortably in her seat. "I wouldn't say that. He had every intention of coming and making you go outside and get some fresh air. Unfortunately, I'm not strong enough to force you to do anything. And it's not babysitting. I'm meeting your agent, who, if he likes my art for your book, could be helpful in my career. Though after what you said at your house, I'm not getting my hopes up. If you're lucky, he'll hate the drawings and you'll be free of me."

Isaac had no idea what she was talking about. And he didn't like the defeated tone in her voice. Delilah was usually full of sass, not unlike Gwenny. "What are you talking about? I haven't seen the drawings yet, but Nash sent some samples to my agent. He loves them."

Lilah pulled off her sunglasses and turned her violet eyes his way. "Then why don't you guys want me to do the art for your book?"

Isaac was getting frustrated again. "Who said that? Nash? Trenton? I know it wasn't Gideon."

Lilah stabbed her index finger into his shoulder. "You did. Not even four hours ago. You said the only reason Nash wants me to do the book is so that we'll spend time together. From the sound of it, Nash thinks you need to get laid, and I'm his choice."

That did it. "Pull the damn car over."

Lilah slapped his hand away from the steering wheel. "Are you trying to get us killed?"

"Get laid, Delilah? Is that what you think?"

Lilah slapped his hand again. "You said Nash was trying to manufacture a romance. I know what men mean when they say romance. They mean sex. Turn on some charm, put on some romantic music, ply the woman with adequate-quality wine, and then get lucky."

Isaac dropped his head into his hands. He wasn't sure how things had gotten so twisted around. Though this was Delilah, after all. She tended to think sideways. "I'm not sure where to start with that statement. Nash is not trying to get me laid. If he were, he wouldn't have picked you. You can barely stand being in the same room with me. Car, too. And for the record, I am not a romantic guy. And I don't play games. If I want a woman, I'm straightforward about it. Which is probably how we got so off track."

"I don't understand.　You said Nash was trying to manufacture a romance."

"He is.　But not how you took it.　First off, we do want you to do the art for the book.　You're very talented, which we saw with the game.　And by taking that talent and applying it to the novels, they will have the same look and feel as the game.　That's what we want.　Second, Nash knows I'm attracted to you.　So he thinks if we spend time together, quality time like working hours together on a book, that you'll eventually reciprocate.　Thirdly, I want to have sex with you, but I would never get you so drunk that you won't say no.　Plenty of women have said no.　You have 'no' written all over your body."

Lilah sputtered.　"Is there a fourth?"

Isaac pointed at the sign.　"You're going to miss your turn."

* * *

Lilah swore under her breath as she quickly made her way over to the exit ramp.　Thankfully the traffic had thinned out as they headed north.　She was so shaken by what Isaac said to her that she didn't think she should be behind the wheel. So she took several deep breaths to help slow the pounding of her heart.　She was torn between ignoring what he said or confronting him.　And why her? She hadn't been nice to him.　She pushed him away when he got too close.　When they worked together, she kept it strictly business.

So she asked the only question she could think of.

"Why?"

Isaac kept his eyes on the road. "Why you?"

She nodded.

"You're smart. You're attractive. You're incredibly talented. As a writer, I can appreciate the skill you have with your art. You were kind to Ginny when we weren't. You take care of your mother with love and compassion. You work hard and put everything you are into your work. You stand your ground when you believe you're right."

Lilah didn't know what to say to that. She wasn't all those things. "Those are some nice rose-colored glasses you're wearing."

Isaac didn't take offense. "Gideon would laugh if he heard that. He would say the opposite. He thinks I'm judgy. Too black and white, and that's coming from a cop."

"You can be judgy. Like when we first met. I wasn't what you expected, was I?"

"No, I don't suppose you were. But to be fair, I wasn't sure what to expect. I figured you'd be younger. I picture tech people in their late teens or early twenties. But I think that's because I'm getting older, and I spend a lot of time teaching that age group. I figured you'd have some piercings or some tattoos. Would wear all black and find the real world beneath you."

Lilah found she could laugh. "You've been watching too much TV. Like any other job, there are all kinds of us. No piercings other than my ears, and no tattoos. And I don't wear all black, as I'm sure you noticed. I was a computer programmer for a couple of years out of college. But I was always into art. I could draw, but I couldn't seem to get the hang of paints. So I began working in graphic design. Most boring job I ever had was with a marketing firm. That's why I left and got into gaming. But that was hard, too. There is all sorts of gender bias. So many men in the gaming industry don't like women on their teams. I figured you for one of those. When we met, you looked me over and dismissed me."

"What?"

Lilah heard his incredulous tone. She was now cruising on a county highway, and the sun was going down. She eased the car onto the shoulder. She flipped on the hazard lights. "You were dismissive."

Isaac turned and crossed his muscular arms over his chest. "I was not."

"I say you were. I've seen that look before. I didn't live up to whatever preconceived notion you had."

Isaac swore. "Delilah, if I did that, I'm sorry. I tend to live in my head. I was in the middle of working through a plot when we met. Trenton was driving me buggy with his storyboards. He was going way off script. Gideon was brooding over Penny, and Nash was rubbing his hands in glee that he'd stolen you from potential competitors. I was annoyed and struggling with the story. I guess I wasn't as friendly as I could have been."

Lilah heard sincerity in his voice. And she wasn't without preconceived notions of her own. She heard "doctor," and it set her on edge. He might not be the medical kind, but he was smart enough to be. When they met, she hadn't known he held multiple doctorate degrees and was fluent in a mind-boggling number of languages.

When she did, he made her feel insecure. The guy was a real-life genius. And she drew what amounted to cartoons. But she didn't say any of that.

Lilah held out a hand. "Truce?"

Isaac, for the first time in days, smiled at her. He took her hand. She glanced down as his much larger hand swallowed hers.

"Truce."

Lilah cleared her throat. "Well, then. We should get going."

Isaac laid a hand over hers that was going to push the ignition button. "And the rest of it?"

"The part where you think you're attracted to me?"

Isaac nodded.

"I don't know. I haven't thought about it."

"I know I'm boring. And I know I tend to lecture. I've seen your eyes glaze over more than once when we talk. No hard feelings. It's my problem. Not yours."

She wanted to argue, but he spoke nothing more than the truth. He did lecture. Probably the professor in him. And she was a terrible student. She'd barely passed her classes since the first grade. She didn't find him boring, exactly. But she had no doubt he'd be bored to tears with her in no time. She wouldn't be able to keep up with his intellect. So no, she couldn't imagine a relationship between them, not even a short one. But by telling her, he'd made it her problem, too.

Isaac pushed the ignition button himself. "Five more hours. Think you can handle it?"

She could and did. They only made one more stop for

gas and the bathroom, and she'd taken a few minutes to put sandwiches together. Isaac hadn't eaten all day, as far as she knew, and the Snickers hadn't stuck long.

When they pulled up to the ski lodge, all she could do was stare. The hotel was nicer than any place she'd stayed before. The building was sided with wood but was very modern in its esthetic. To top it off, there was a beautiful view of the snowcapped mountains behind it. "Wow."

Isaac got out of the car. He met the young man who came to get their luggage.

Lilah was still struck by the beauty of the hotel and the view. She barely heard what Isaac was saying until he took her arm. The bellhop behind them was rolling their luggage along. She'd never stayed in a place that had a bellhop before. She was startled when a key card was pressed into her hand.

Isaac took her hand, and they followed the bellhop inside. "Don't be shocked when you go in. Nash only stays in the best suites."

Despite the warning, she was shocked. She'd swear the room was bigger than her and her mom's apartment. The carpet was plush, and the sitting area was massive. There was a fireplace lit, a large-screen television not so discreetly hanging on the wall, a mini kitchen, and an office area. There were two doors.

Isaac tipped the bellhop and closed the door. "You can have whichever bedroom you like. If I were you, I'd take the one on the left. Has a much nicer view."

Lilah realized what Isaac had meant when he said don't be shocked. "We're sharing a suite?"

Isaac grabbed her suitcase and headed for the room on the left. "It was supposed to be for Nash and me, remember? But there are two bedrooms, each with its own bath. You'll have full privacy."

The bedroom was done in creams and golds. The plush carpet from the living area continued on. She peeked into the bathroom. There was a huge spa tub, an oversized shower, and a huge vanity with two sinks. The bed was a king and took up the center of the room. The curtains were open to a view of the mountains. "Wow."

Isaac set her suitcase down. "So you said. Nash doesn't do anything in half measures. It's the best or nothing. My head hurts. I'm going to lay down. It's been a long day. There is a dining area downstairs, or you can have food sent up. Charge everything to the room."

Lilah bit her lip as Isaac left. She saw him grab his duffle and suitcase and take them to the other room. She followed.

Isaac stopped when he would have closed the door in her face. "Want to make sure I was telling the truth about the view?"

Lilah came in. The room looked just like hers. The view wasn't quite as nice, though still lovely. But that wasn't why she followed. "Drugs in your duffle?"

Isaac sat on the bed. "Probably."

Lilah opened the bag and rummaged around. She stopped, somewhat shocked, when she found a box of condoms at the bottom of the bag.

Isaac lay down, not seeing what she was doing. "Trenton is a terrible packer. Find them yet?"

Clearing her throat, she pushed the box back to the bottom. She then found a bag that sounded like there were pills in it. She found his prescription for the headaches and shook a pill out. "Let me get some water."

Isaac pointed back to the living area. "There will be bottled water in the fridge."

She found it, uncapped it, and handed the water and pill to him.

"Thanks, Delilah."

She left the room and closed the door behind her. She had heard from Trenton that the neurologist Isaac was seeing warned him about headaches. The right eye was severely damaged, and there was nerve damage, not only in the eye but in the face. Trenton was the one who drove Isaac to and from appointments, and she'd seen the pain on Trenton's face every time he came back from one of them. When she'd asked if Isaac had any family to take him, Trenton had simply said there was no one. The quartet was his family.

Restless, Lilah took the room key and went in search of the lounge. As she strolled through the hotel, she became more uncomfortable. The men and women having a late-night dinner were well-dressed. She was sure the woman seated at the bar was wearing silk. She should have realized any place Nash would stay was not one where she would fit in.

She took a seat at the bar. Mindful that it wasn't her money she was spending, she ordered an inexpensive glass of white wine and a bowl of clam chowder.

A young woman took a seat next to her. "Thank

goodness there is another woman here. I've been dodging men all night. I'm Grace."

Lilah could see why. The younger woman had dark hair, milky skin, and wore a low-cut dress with her assets on full display. Her makeup was perfect, the colors flattering. "I'm Delilah."

"What a sweet name. Are you here alone?"

Lilah took a sip of her wine while Grace waved the bartender over. "No. I'm here with someone. Sort of."

Grace ordered a drink Lilah had never heard of, while flashing an impressive diamond on her left finger. Lilah asked the question the woman was obviously trying to get her to ask. "Are you with someone?"

"Not anymore. Martin and I had a terrible fight. He's off somewhere, probably drowning his sorrows."

Lilah pointed to the ring. "Husband?"

"Mmm. No, fiancé. Or we were until we had a terrible fight. But he'll come around. He always does. So you're sort of here with someone?"

Lilah didn't doubt that Martin would come crawling back. Grace looked like a woman who would make a man beg. "He's sort of my boss. But when we drove up tonight, he said he was attracted to me."

Grace let out a practiced, musical laugh. "I can see why. Men are attracted to red heads. Women, too. What I wouldn't give to have your hair. Just lovely."

Lilah pulled back when the woman touched her hair.

Grace smiled and didn't comment. "Well, I suppose I should take my drink back to my room. We'll see if Martin is waiting."

Lilah gave her a small smile, grateful that she was leaving. Lilah finished her meal in silence and signed the check to charge to the room.

Lilah took her time going back to the room. The hotel was lovely. There was an Olympic-sized swimming pool, a workout room with another pool, and a spa area where you could get pampered. She thought Isaac might benefit from a massage. With all he'd been through, it would do him good to relax.

She passed through the front of the hotel. In the distance were the ski slopes. She had never been skiing. She would bet Nash and Isaac were good at it. For all of Isaac's bookish looks, she knew he was fit. She'd seen the muscles for herself. Though at the time, that wasn't what she'd been focused on. She'd been trying to help save Isaac's life. But in hindsight, she remembered well the muscled chest and arms as his shirt had been removed to keep the ammonia from soaking into his skin. She felt a slight stirring in her belly at the remembered sight.

Shaking her unruly thoughts away, she headed to their suite. Romance and men had been so low on her priority list that they'd pretty much fallen off. Isaac's declaration that he found her attractive had shaken her. She didn't even want to think about his frank statement that he wanted to have sex with her. She didn't see any of the quartet as relationship candidates. They had unknowingly rescued her from losing her apartment. She had been drowning in medical bills when she'd met them. In the past year, she'd gotten back on solid footing. And with Trenton's help, she even had some savings. She treated all four of them like the brothers she never had.

Well, she supposed Isaac was an exception. She'd treated him like the unwanted brother. He intimidated her. He made her feel like a gawky teenager again. And it wasn't a pleasant feeling. But he said he was attracted to her. She didn't know what, if anything, she should do about that. She had been honest when she said she hadn't thought about him that way. Men asked her out from time to time. She'd had relationships. She was thirty-one, after all. He said it was his problem, not hers. But it felt like her problem, too. And now that she knew, she wasn't sure what to think.

Lilah opened her purse and searched for the room key. She knew she'd put it in the pocket. She opened the purse further, but there was no key. She looked behind her to see if she might have dropped it. Frustrated, she leaned on the door while she started to dump her purse. The door swung open behind her, dropping her onto her backside.

Cursing under her breath, she rolled to her knees and stood. She knew she hadn't left the door open. On the table, she saw the key. Realizing what had happened, she rushed to Isaac's room. She flung his door open. His duffle bag was zipped where she'd left it, and his suitcase was standing next to the bathroom door. She saw his pants lying in the middle of the floor, probably where he'd kicked them off. His wallet was lying beside the pants. She dropped to her knees. There was a credit card, his driver's license, his insurance card, and a few business cards. Inside the billfold, there was no cash. Closing her eyes, she realized how stupid she'd been. Grace had no doubt lifted the key card from her purse. She set his wallet on the table and went to her room. Nothing in her room looked disturbed. But when she got to the bathroom, her toiletry bag had been dumped. She didn't have anything valuable with her. No doubt other women at the hotel had plenty of jewelry, expensive perfumes, and other valuables.

Lilah then went to her suitcase. Inside it, her laptop was still there. Sighing with relief, she pulled it out of the suitcase and put it in the safe. For good measure, she tossed her purse in there. Knowing she had no choice but to wake him, she went back to Isaac's room.

She knew Isaac hated taking the pills because they made him drowsy. He was on his back snoring softly. He'd stripped down to an undershirt, and she was guessing his underwear. His shirt was tossed on the other side of the room.

She came to the side of the bed. "Isaac?"

His head turned her way, but his eyes didn't open.

She laid a hand on his shoulder. "Isaac."

His eyes shot open, and his body tensed. Recognition followed. "Delilah. What is it?"

Lilah licked her lips. "Someone broke into the room. A woman."

Isaac sat up and grabbed his glasses off the nightstand. "Are you sure?"

Lilah flushed in embarrassment. "I'm sure. I was having dinner and this woman sat down next to me. She seemed harmless. Said she'd had a fight with her fiancé. But when I came back to the room, the key wasn't in my purse. And the door was open. The key was lying on the table. Your wallet was lying next to your pants. I don't know if anything was taken, but your credit card is there."

Isaac swore. He climbed out of bed and turned the lamp on. He grabbed his wallet where Lilah had put it on the dresser. "Cash is gone. Wonder why she didn't take the card?"

Lilah was very aware that Isaac wore nothing but an undershirt and a sexy pair of gray boxer briefs. He didn't seem to notice he was half naked. Trying not to stare, Lilah pointed to her room. "I had my purse, and she didn't lift anything but the key card. She went through my toiletries, but I didn't have anything worth stealing. She left my laptop in the bag."

Isaac grabbed his pants and yanked them over his long legs. "I'll go talk to the front desk. But it's not likely she'll be caught."

"I know what she looks like. So does the bartender."

Isaac grabbed his shirt and put it on but didn't bother to button it. "And she'll look like every other woman here. She'll have worn nice clothes, have nice hair, wear too much makeup, and look a little too desperate."

Lilah supposed he had a point. "I suppose I'm the one who stood out. Even she commented on my hair, though I think she might have been hitting on me. Or pretending to."

Isaac searched the rest of his things, but nothing else seemed to be missing. He glanced at the table. "My watch is gone."

Lilah knew well the gold watch Isaac wore. It was a large timepiece, solid gold with diamonds for numbers. "I'm so sorry, Isaac. That watch had to be expensive. I didn't think something like this could happen in a place like this."

Isaac took her hand while he slipped his feet into his shoes without socks. He led her out of the room and grabbed the key card. "It was very expensive, no doubt. Nash bought it. It was a birthday present. And things like this can happen anywhere."

Lilah trailed behind him as they went to the front desk. The hotel manager was apologetic and offered his sympathies. Lilah noticed he didn't offer to call the police. He did offer to comp the room for the night and move them to a different room. Isaac declined the room change and told him to make it two nights.

Lilah wanted to argue, but Isaac took her hand and led her back to their room. He firmly shut the door behind them and locked it.

"Why didn't you call the police? She stole your money and watch. You can't let her get away with it."

Isaac went to the mini bar and poured two small glasses of some gold liquid she didn't want to drink. "It's not worth calling the police. She's long gone by now. In the end, she got an expensive watch and a couple hundred bucks. It's not like the insurance company is going to pay me the value of the stolen watch. You said nothing of yours was stolen, so like I said, it's not worth the hassle. After what happened six months ago, a stolen watch doesn't seem like such a big deal."

Lilah shivered. He had a point. Nothing like chemical burns and having a gun pointed at you to put life into perspective. Her problem was she was anticipating a good night's sleep. She thought she was safe behind the locked doors of the hotel, and she didn't have to worry about her mother. At least, not as much. She'd gotten a text message earlier that she was fine and enjoying the trip. But now this had happened.

"I should let you go back to sleep. I can see the headache is worse."

Isaac simply guided her to the sofa and handed her the drink. "It will help settle your nerves."

Lilah took a sip, and her mouth puckered and then burned. "What is it?"

Isaac watched with amusement as she took another sip. "Bourbon. If it's not to your taste, I can get you something else."

Lilah finished it but shuddered. "No thanks. I think this might eat a hole in my stomach."

Isaac emptied his glass in one swallow. "It's getting late. We should both go to bed."

Lilah could feel the heat of the liquor going straight to her head. "I don't usually drink hard drinks like that."

Isaac stood and pulled her to her feet. "I could smell wine on your breath earlier. I should have poured you a glass of that."

Lilah looked up at Isaac. "Bourbon was fine. Might take some getting used to. But I am sorry. And I'm really sorry about your watch. You can't replace the sentimental value."

Isaac touched a finger to her cheek. "Nash only bought it because he said it might keep me from being late all the time. And since I refuse to buy a smartphone, he bought the watch because it cost more than a smartphone and because you can set it to beep. I get into my work so much that sometimes I lose track of time."

"Then I owe Nash an apology the next time you're late."

Isaac gazed down at her. He'd pulled off his glasses, so her face was blurry. "Delilah, please go to bed now. You can continue apologizing in the morning."

Lilah saw the heat forming in his gaze. His one eye was still cloudy and would likely always be that way. But his other eye was a brilliant blue as it gazed down at her. She knew if she stayed where she was, he would kiss her.

Confused, Lilah fled to her bedroom and closed the door behind her.

Chapter Four

Isaac sat at the table with his laptop reading his emails. After he'd gone back to his room, he'd emailed an old friend of his, one he hadn't talked to in fifteen years. Since the attack and the press surrounding it had gone national, Isaac had been on his guard. While the intruder last night could have been a coincidence, Isaac wasn't a big believer in coincidences. He did believe in history repeating itself. His old friend Monroe's reply assured him there was nothing to worry about and that nothing out of the ordinary was on his radar. He said the woman was likely nothing more than an average con artist. It made Isaac feel better, but no less wary.

For the past six months, he'd been watching and waiting. And while the watch and the money ticked him off, he didn't want the police involved. He'd messaged Gideon about what happened, and Gideon said much the same as his old friend did. Just another hustler who saw Delilah and figured she was a good mark. And unfortunately, the woman was right.

But what continued to nag at him was that Delilah wasn't a good mark, not if the goal was to rob her hotel room. The hotel was filled with well-dressed people wearing jewelry more expensive than his watch. Delilah stood out in her worn, baggy clothes. Nothing about her screamed money.

He poured another cup of coffee and sat back at his computer and got back to work. Delilah had thankfully set everything up on his laptop so that it was saved in the cloud. He hadn't lost any of his work when his laptop died. Frustrated, he worked on the edits of his first graphic novel. He much preferred to print his books and edit them by hand, but the hotel office didn't have a printer. Just his luck, they sent all receipts via email.

He was taking a sip when Delilah came out of her bedroom. Her hair was wet and hanging around her shoulders. He could tell she'd put some makeup on; her freckles weren't as noticeable. Nor were the dark circles he knew were under her eyes.

Lilah crossed to the kitchen and poured herself a cup of coffee. "Good morning, Isaac."

Isaac watched her as she leaned against the counter. Her feet were bare and her toenails were painted turquoise. He didn't think he'd ever seen her in bare feet. He'd also never seen her in a skirt or a dress, though he'd certainly like to. Today she had on her usual faded jeans and a slouchy yellow sweater. Her lavender eyes were watching him.

Isaac pushed the chair opposite him out with his foot. "Why not join me? I've been working on the book this morning. My agent should be here in a couple of hours. He's not a morning person."

Lilah took a seat. "I'm usually up early. Once the sun is up, I'm up."

Isaac went back to his book, though his focus was shot. "My body rhythms were messed up while my eyes were healing. When day and night blur, it's hard to keep to normal sleep patterns. Thankfully that's been getting better with my left eye mostly back to normal."

Lilah tucked her foot under her leg. "Besides Nash, you were the first one at the office. Nash says you're learning to drive again."

Isaac grunted. "Doc sent me to an occupational therapist who is helping me learn to do things with only one eye. Eventually I'll go back to teaching, but I want to be comfortable driving again first."

Lilah smiled at him, her eyes soft as she looked at him. "That's great. I know you like teaching. But if I could write like you, I'd do it full time. I tried writing children's books in college. I thought it was a great idea and I could do the illustrations, but I wasn't very good at it. I had the story in pictures, but I couldn't put it down in words. I admire you and Ginny for that."

That piqued Isaac's interest. "Still have them? The books?"

Lilah finished her coffee. "Probably. Want a refill?"

Isaac got up and took her cup. "I'll do it. You do enough for me already."

After coffee and a light breakfast were delivered to their room, they fell back into their normal routines. Isaac worked on the edits of the novel, and Lilah pulled out her sketch pad and pencils.

A loud knock on the door an hour later disrupted both of them. Isaac glanced at the door. "Stefan, no doubt."

A flurry of French filled the room as the robust man entered. The man topped maybe five and a half feet. Lilah, at five-six, was taller. Isaac, whom she would put at six feet even, towered over him. The man's waist was straining the belt that cinched the expensive and no doubt tailored pants over his ample form. His obviously black-dyed hair gleamed in the light.

Isaac answered in kind, the language flowing naturally from his tongue. He then switched to English. "Stefan, meet Delilah Fitzpatrick."

The man took her hand and kissed it with a flourish. "Irish, I see. I had wondered when Isaac told me your name. I can see your temperament in your work. Just amazing."

Isaac couldn't help but smile at Lilah's dazed expression. The older man had already done two turns around the room and admired every aspect of the space, from the carpet to the small chandelier that added soft lighting to the room.

The man, without an ounce of self-control, snatched Lilah's sketch pad from the table. Another flurry of French exploded from him.

Lilah looked at Isaac. "Is that good or bad?"

Isaac responded. "Good. He loves it when he gets to use his French."

The man pointed at Isaac. "This one is good. Very good. He translates his own books. Best client I have."

Isaac gestured to the table. "No doubt you say that to all your clients."

"Mmm. This I like. I like very much." He tossed the sketchbook on the table. "When do I get to see it together?"

Lilah took a seat and pulled up what she'd transferred to the computer so far. She had already started assembling the book. "It's easier for me to edit on the laptop."

Isaac peered over her shoulder. "She hasn't let me look yet."

Lilah waved her hand at Isaac in dismissal. "It's easier for me to edit the images when I have Isaac's story at hand. But the images are not completely done yet."

The man dropped into a chair and spun her laptop, so he had full view. He then waved them away. "Go find something to do."

Isaac grabbed his and Lilah's coats from where he'd hung them. "Come on. He won't move for a couple of hours. And he hates an audience when he works."

Lilah turned nervous eyes toward the man. She whispered to Isaac. "We're just supposed to leave him alone with our work?"

Isaac held her coat and helped her into it. "It's best this way."

He took her hand and exited the room. "Nash wanted me to get some fresh air. We can honestly say we did."

He kept her hand in his until they were outside. He handed her his gloves. "I noticed you weren't wearing any."

Lilah tugged on the oversized gloves, but not until after Isaac pulled out a second pair. "It's cold, but it's different somehow."

Isaac took her hand again and walked them to the trail that led to the ski slopes. "There is something about Vermont air. It's clean and crisp. D.C. has its charm, but a winter day is not always one of them."

Lilah pulled her hood over her head but kept her hand in his. "Do you come here a lot?"

Isaac turned them toward the tree line. "I used to come a couple of times during the season. Trenton has his boat. I have the slopes. Or I did."

Lilah squeezed his hand. "You're learning to drive with

one eye. You could learn to ski with just one, too."

Isaac tried to brush off his sudden melancholy mood. "Skiing is different. It requires full concentration. Believe it or not, I wanted to do it professionally. Visions of grandeur, no doubt, but when I was sixteen, I had visions of becoming an Olympic champion. But while I was good, I wasn't quite good enough for the Olympics. What about you, Delilah? What did you want to be?"

Lilah gripped his hand tighter as they made their way over a slippery section of the path. "I always wanted to be an artist. I tried painting and sculpting. I even tried stained glass. But like I said before, I wasn't good with paints. My sculpting wasn't bad, but I wasn't ever going to be rich doing it. I still dabble from time to time. And I wasn't quite as coordinated as I needed to be to work with glass. I still have scars on my hands. My mother has my one and only attempt at it hanging in the kitchen window. So I drew. A lot. Took a little time, but I got good at it. Then I discovered computers. I was fascinated by what you could do with one. In college, I did a computer animated series for a class. The college television station picked it up and played it for a time."

Isaac put his arm around her waist to steady her. He often forgot she limped. "Is this trek too much?"

Lilah shook her head. "No, I just have a fear of falling."

Isaac tightened his hold and they continued on. "So why didn't you keep doing animation?"

"I don't know. It was fun, but when I ran out of ideas, I quit. I had done twenty of them over four years. But after a while, I wanted to do something different. The story had run its course, I guess, and I didn't want to do another cartoon. That's when I made graphic design my career. Then I got into coding. I'm excited about the graphic novels. I don't have to come up with the story, just the art. I'll add that I sucked at marketing. I couldn't make myself care about the product I was supposed to be trying to sell. I managed to keep my job for a year before they finally let me go."

Isaac wanted to keep her talking. He'd learned more about her in the last twenty minutes than he had since he'd met her. "So then onto gaming. You're good at it. Very good."

"Must seem silly to you."

Isaac didn't like her sudden change in attitude. "It's not silly. If you'll recall, I wrote the book that Cantwell is based on."

Lilah pulled away. "Yeah, but writing the novel isn't the same. I mean, your agent said you translate your own books. You teach literature and history. I've lost count of how many doctorates Nash says you have. You spoke to your agent like French is your first language. And Nash says your IQ is like two hundred."

He answered without thinking. "Two hundred and five."

She shoved her gloved hands into her pockets. "See what I mean?"

Isaac stopped. "It's just a number. There are lots of people with high IQs, Delilah. But it's what you do with your life, what you choose to do with what you have, that matters. There are a lot of smart and lazy people out there who will never reach their full potential. I see it with my students sometimes. They lack motivation."

Lilah started walking again.

"Delilah, please."

Her head dropped and her hood hid her face. She stopped. "I've been trying to figure out since yesterday what you could possibly see in me. You're successful. You have a talent I can only dream of having. All of your friends are successful. Just look at Nash and Trenton. Even Gideon, though he's not rich. I bet you date brainiacs. And one day you're going to get married and have genius children."

Isaac held out his hand to her. He didn't budge until she took it. "Two geniuses don't necessarily have genius children. And two average people can have a genius kid. It's still one of the great mysteries of the human brain. It's not like eye color or hair color you inherit. I could give you more details, but your eyes are likely to glaze over again."

It didn't get past him that she didn't argue the point.

Lilah didn't drop the other subject. She tipped her face up to see him. "But you do date smart women, don't you?"

Isaac thought there was a trap somewhere in that question. But he had a feeling his answer could determine the path of their relationship. "A lot of the women I date I meet through work-related conferences, or women Nash introduces me to. So, yeah, some of them probably qualify as geniuses. Some of them were real airheads, to use a colloquial term. Some were pretty; some were beautiful. But I've changed. I'm not interested in IQs like I might have been ten years ago. And I'm interested in more than a woman's bust size, unlike the teenager I was. I want someone who I can love and marry, and someone who wants to do the same. I'm no longer interested in affairs or casual dating. So I guess my requirements in a woman are a lot different than they used to be the closer to forty I get. You're the type of woman who loves. I see it in all the things you do for your mom. I saw it when you helped Ginny. And I think you aren't opposed to marriage. Maybe marriage to someone like me, but not the concept of it. But like I said, it's not your problem. It's mine."

"I'm really starting to hate that phrase. It's very much my problem. You can't tell a woman you're attracted to her, that you think about sex with her, and expect her to just brush it off."

Isaac tugged her back toward the ski slopes. "You'd be surprised how many women can and do just brush it off."

Lilah's brows furrowed. "How many women have you told that you're attracted to them and want to have sex with them?"

"I prefer honesty. If I'm attracted, I say so. You might be the first woman I so bluntly told that I wanted to have sex with her, but it's more than that. It's the whole package. You had me frustrated. I'm usually more eloquent and more tactful in my approach with women."

Lilah threw up her free hand. "You used the word 'colloquial' in a sentence, and you weren't teaching a history lesson. Honestly, Isaac, I don't understand you."

He felt his stomach drop. "No, I don't suppose you do."

Lilah yanked him to a halt. "Okay, let's try something else."

Before Isaac could ask what that something else was, Lilah tossed her hood back, threw her arms around his neck, pulled his head down to hers, and planted a firm kiss on his lips. Stunned, he just stood there.

Lilah kept her grip on his neck. "I think we need to try that again."

Isaac's mind went blank when Lilah kissed him again. Without thought, he wrapped his arms around her waist, gripped her so tight her feet left the ground, and devoured her mouth. She tasted as sweet as he'd fantasized she would, but with a hint of her toothpaste. Helpless to stop himself, he tasted the seam of her lips. When she didn't protest, he used his tongue to open her mouth to his. His hands left her waist. His mouth broke contact with hers for only a moment as she dropped back to the ground, but his hands dove into her mass of red hair, and he kissed her again.

He'd heard the phrase time standing still, but he'd never experienced it before. This interlude with Lilah felt like it lasted forever. But when she planted her hands firmly on his chest and pushed, he released her. Her lavender eyes were dazed, her lips ruby red. He touched his thumb to her swollen lips before letting her go. He stood still and waited for the verdict.

Lilah touched trembling fingers to her lips. "Jeez."

Trust Delilah to give him an ambivalent answer. He glanced back toward the hotel. "We should head back. Stefan is probably almost done."

"What? Oh, right, your agent. Sure. By all means, let's head back."

Isaac took her hand to keep her steady as they walked back. The trip back didn't take nearly as long as the trip out. Lilah kept a tight grip on his hand, and her pace was brisk.

When they entered the hotel room, Stefan was back to his previous form. He kissed both of her cheeks, kept his words in French, and then punched Isaac in the shoulder. Then the man left the room in a rush, much as he had come in earlier.

Lilah stared at the door. "Your agent is very intense. I take it the kiss on the cheeks and the shoulder punch were his way of saying he liked it."

Isaac went to the wine fridge and pulled out a small bottle of sparkling champagne. "That, my Delilah, was his very enthusiastic way of saying he loved it. He's going to go back to his hotel and work on the contract. He has no doubt he can sell the novels to the same publisher that bought Cantwell, and he wants you under contract. Trust me when I say the deal Stefan comes back with will please both of us. He's one of the few people I know who doesn't play games. He's willing to fight to get his talent what they're worth. I did tell him to get you an advance when the publisher signs. Cantwell will continue to pay you for the work you do on the game, but the book deal will pay you for your work on the book. And given how crazy things have been for you this past year, I thought you'd appreciate it."

Isaac poured the sparkling champagne into a small wine glass he pulled from the bar. He handed her a glass. He then tapped his glass to hers. "Congrats, Delilah."

* * *

The next day, Lilah was still dazed. She and Isaac had gone back to work after Stefan left. Then when it was dark, they headed to the hotel's restaurant for dinner. He'd plied her with enough food and wine that when they got back to the hotel room, she'd fallen asleep on the oversized sofa while Isaac had been reading a book. She tried, but failed, to ignore the fact that the book was not in English. She couldn't say one way or another what the language was. And she'd opted not to ask.

She still wasn't sure what shocked her more, the fact that she was going to be published or the fact that Isaac had kissed her like he was a man starving. She was pretty sure the kiss won that contest. She had meant to give him a light kiss. She wanted to see if there might, just might, be something more to come from their budding relationship. She thought if she kissed him, she'd know if she could be attracted to him. And boy, was she.

She knew she found him attractive. He was handsome, despite the scars. She loved the precision cut of his sandy blond hair. He was fit and dressed well. He spoke well and had good manners. Despite his tendency to lecture, there was a lot to like about him. And if all that wasn't enough, the man could cook. He often fed her when she was at his house.

So here she was, walking the indoor track at the hotel's gym, trying to sort out her emotions. Isaac had told her he was going swimming. She wasn't comfortable exposing her legs, not to him or anyone else, so she had left him to it. She'd grabbed a pair of sweatpants that she slept in and an old t-shirt. She had been honest when she said she was afraid of falling. She didn't pay attention to her limp much, but the fear of falling was very real.

Lilah kept her pace brisk. If only he weren't so smart. She never told anyone how much she struggled with school. She'd barely scraped by high school. In college, she had to have a tutor, and even then, she'd barely passed. Her associate degree was another thing her mother kept in a frame and out in the open. Her mother often told her how proud of her she was. Lilah was proud, too, but she decided not to go for her bachelor's degree. By the time she'd finally gotten her degree, she'd moved into computers, and she had a handful of certificates that were enough to keep her employed.

She didn't know how to tell Isaac she had a learning disability. Because of the time she spent in and out of the hospital trying to fix her legs, her dyslexia had gone undiagnosed. Her parents just thought she was behind on her studies. And she was behind. But when she'd gotten into the eighth grade, a teacher of hers finally figured it out. Her parents had tried, but tutors were expensive. When she turned eighteen, she refused to keep seeing the specialist. It was money she simply could not afford to keep shelling out. In her opinion, she'd learned enough to get by.

Isaac and his incredible intellect intimidated her. Ginny had once asked her why she didn't like Isaac. But the truth was, deep down inside, she did like him. And after the way he kissed her, she couldn't pretend she wasn't attracted to him. But he wanted a permanent relationship. Or at least one that could become permanent. He wanted to get married and have children. Lilah didn't think she was the right person for him. And while she knew he was right that two geniuses didn't equal a genius child, it probably increased the chances significantly.

Less than an hour before the attack that took his vision, she had overheard Isaac telling Trenton that he wanted to settle down and have a family. So it hadn't come as a surprise to her that Isaac was looking for more than an affair. She just never imagined he had her in mind. She couldn't think of even one time he'd looked at her in a way that indicated he was attracted. Or maybe his intense face was his attracted face. The thought made her heart beat faster. That look was one that she was more than a little familiar with.

She did one final lap before she stopped. Her leg was aching, a sure sign it was time to stop. Unable to help herself, she made her way to the nearby pool. Isaac was doing laps. It was hard to see details under the water, but she could tell he was only wearing swim trunks. She could see his muscular arms as they propelled him through the water. She took a seat and watched.

She lost count of the number of laps he did before he finally hauled himself out of the pool. She stared at his mostly naked body as the water dripped off him. She had seen him in just his underwear not two days ago, but this was different. This time her palms itched to touch, and she wanted to kiss every water droplet from his fantastic chest.

Isaac saw her while he was reaching for his towel and glasses. He draped the towel over his back and shoulders after putting his glasses on so he could see her. "Done with your walk?"

Lilah swallowed and tried to ignore how his athletic swim shorts clung to his body. "Yeah. I came to see if you wanted breakfast."

He watched her for a moment; a small smile tipped the corners of his mouth. "Let me take a shower, and we can eat."

Lilah watched as he walked toward the men's locker room. The back view was as nice as the front. She closed her eyes. Attracted? Yeah, she was attracted all right. Now she had to figure out how to tamp it down. Because if he kissed her again, she wasn't sure she could resist. Wasn't sure she'd want to. And if he asked for more, she didn't know what she'd do.

Chapter Five

The next two days flew by. Isaac managed to keep his hands and mouth to himself. And sadly, she hadn't thrown herself at him. He and Delilah had focused on work. And when Stefan showed up with the contract and a check, Delilah's mouth dropped open. Isaac had given her an "I told you so" look and watched with satisfaction as she signed her name on the contract. She was now obligated to do three books with him. There was plenty of time to make Delilah fall in love with him.

Now they were packing up the SUV. Delilah's mom would be gone for another week, and he had hopes he could spend time with Delilah that didn't involve work. They had taken time each day to get the fresh air he'd promised Nash he'd get, but she had been reserved and had said little. When they got back to D.C., they could start with dinner out, maybe the theater, or perhaps she'd like the conservatory. He'd been spending some of his time learning to play computer games in an attempt to learn more about the market. Maybe she'd be interested in teaching him how to play. But whatever they did, he vowed to stay far away from libraries, museums, or the university.

Lilah tossed her bag in and waited for Isaac to shut the door. "Want to drive for a little while? We'll be on some rural roads. Nothing but forest for a good part of it."

Isaac thought about it and nodded. "In the summer, we can go camping out here. This part of the state has a lot of hiking trails and campgrounds. In the winter, there's hardly anyone around, outside of the ski resorts. Nash likes this one because it's the most remote, and people rarely recognize him."

"I didn't. Recognize him, I mean." Lilah gave a light laugh and climbed into the passenger seat and buckled her seat belt.

"That's because you're not an obsessive social climber. Anyone who wants to be, or thinks they are somebody, tries to latch onto Nash. One of these days I half expect him to ditch D.C. But his family and friends all live there, so he settles for short vacations like this one. Had he come, he would not have worked."

Lilah watched as he swapped glasses. "I can't picture Nash camping. Or Trenton. Gideon maybe. Does he come with?"

"Actually, Trenton will as long as there's water. He likes to kayak and water ski. I can usually tempt Gideon if for no other reason than to unwind."

Isaac dropped silent as he concentrated on the roads. He hadn't practiced driving much, though the occupational therapist had been encouraging him. It was nice to be behind the wheel of his SUV. The vehicle wasn't just for show. He liked going off-road and off the beaten path when he camped. Today, he kept to the main roads. The sun was covered by clouds, and within twenty minutes, snow started to fall. It wasn't much, but it made him extra cautious.

Lilah was chatting about the book when he saw a black SUV coming up on him. He recognized the license plate from one he'd seen at the hotel. The hairs on the back of his neck stood up. To the right of them, there was a drop-off, and woods to the left. It didn't get more isolated than that.

Isaac tuned her out. The SUV sped closer. "Delilah. Tighten your seat belt."

Lilah didn't get a chance to respond. The SUV came up fast and slammed into him as it came around a curve.

Isaac heard her scream but didn't look at her. With his right hand, he grabbed the base of her seat belt and yanked it tight across her lap. He did the same with his. He grabbed the wheel with both hands as the SUV slammed into them again. He managed to keep the vehicle on the road. He couldn't get a good look at the driver, but when he saw a pistol come out of the window of the passenger side, he pushed Lilah down so that her head wasn't visible. She tried to fight him, but he was stronger than she was. The driver slammed into him again, and his SUV fishtailed.

Isaac cursed as he saw another curve ahead. The passenger aimed and shot out his rear tire. Struggling to keep control, the other SUV slammed into them again as he hit the turn. The road surface was covered in a dusting of snow despite the canopy of the trees. Isaac tried but failed to keep the SUV steady. Between the wet road and the flat tire, he spun out and hit the railing hard enough to break through it and went over the edge.

The force of the SUV hitting the ground jarred him, but he managed to keep his hands on the wheel. He tried but couldn't brake. The momentum from the vehicle on the wet leaves just made him skid as he pumped the brakes. Instead, he tried to steer. He couldn't grab Lilah from where she was now partially wedged under the dash from when he bent her over. But he couldn't focus on her. He needed to steer clear of the trees. He turned the SUV so that his side of the vehicle scraped the trees as the vehicle slid. After a few attempts to slow the vehicle down, the vehicle came up to a hill, hit a small boulder, and finally stopped with a loud boom and the sound of twisted metal.

Breathing heavily and afraid for Delilah, he undid his seat belt. He tried to undo hers, but the mechanism was stuck. He opened the glove box and pulled out his hunting knife and his Glock 19. He tucked the pistol into his coat pocket and used the knife to slice through her seat belt. Her body slid, and he was rewarded with a groan.

He carefully pulled Delilah back fully onto the seat. There was a gash in the back of her head. He looked behind him and saw that his duffle bag had jostled to the rear seat. He managed to hold onto Delilah while prying the bag open. He grabbed the first piece of cloth that came to hand. He pressed it to the back of her head and managed to get her upright.

"Come on, sweetheart, open your eyes."

Lilah came to with a start. "Isaac."

He held her when she latched onto him, her face pressed to his chest inside his coat. The sun was still hidden behind the clouds, and it was hard to see up the hill they'd come down. He realized his glasses had come off and everything was fuzzy. He found the pair smashed on the dash. He pulled the cracked lenses on anyway. He could barely make out the vehicle at the top of the hill. It was nothing more than a black blur, but it was there. Isaac remained where he was, with Delilah against his chest, as he simply watched.

They were too far away for the driver to see them inside the vehicle. No doubt they were waiting to see if the door opened.

Isaac kept Delilah against his chest, crooning soft words in her ear until the vehicle finally left. They were obviously not going to risk climbing down the treacherous hill to see if they were dead. They were damn lucky they weren't. If they'd had a head-on collision with a tree, it was likely neither of them would be breathing right now.

Lilah finally pulled away, her body trembling in the aftereffects of the crash. "What happened? Why would they do that?"

Isaac was pretty sure he knew the answer. "Let's sit you up so I can take a look at you. What hurts?"

He turned Delilah in her seat, and she cried out. He glanced down. Her foot was turned unnaturally sideways. He cursed, then again. He carefully eased her back to face forward.

Tears fell down her cheeks. "My head hurts. And I think my leg is broken."

He needed to free her so he could get a better idea of what they were dealing with. He could tell she was struggling to stem her tears, but they kept falling down her ashen cheeks. He took her hand and pressed it against the back of her head where he was still holding the fabric to her cut. "Press. Really hard. I need to see your leg."

She did as she was told and watched him with pain-filled eyes as he left the vehicle and came around her side. He had to slam into the door a couple of times to loosen it to open it.

Her voice was steady but still choked with tears. "How bad?"

He wanted to lie and tell her it was fine. But it wasn't. "It's going to hurt when I move you. But I've got to see what we're dealing with."

She whimpered and bit her lip, but she didn't cry out as he freed her leg. He managed to get her seat pushed back all the way so he could get better access to her leg. There wasn't any blood on her leg, which was a good sign. He took his hunting knife and cut a slit in her jeans. The skin hadn't broken, but it was as bad as he feared. Her ankle was out of place, no doubt broken. And he could see the spot under her skin and muscle where the bone was broken. He noticed faded scars on her calf but didn't ask about them.

Isaac pulled his phone out of his pocket. He swore. He grabbed Lilah's phone where it lay on the floor. Cursing some more, he tossed the phone on the dash and went back to her leg. "No signal."

Lilah looked down. His head obstructed her view. "You're going to need to try to straighten it. I know what to do."

Isaac glanced up at her. "First let's get you in the back. I can lay the seats down. It will be easier to get to your leg that way."

Isaac tossed their luggage and cooler on the ground and laid the back seat down so he could stretch Lilah out. It would be a tight fit, but she could lie at an angle to keep her leg straight. It took Isaac a few minutes to maneuver her out of the front seat and get her into the back. They were both sweating by the time he got her settled. He used her duffle bag as a pillow, with her legs facing him. He contemplated the suitcase on the ground. The plastic handles on his suitcase would have to do to immobilize her leg.

It took a little work, but he managed to cut and break the handles off his suitcase. He then grabbed his duffle and rummaged for the smaller bag Trenton had packed. Shaking his head, but glad Trenton had tossed them in, Isaac pulled out the bottle of pain killers. He hadn't taken them in months, but they would help Delilah. The cooler was still filled with water, tea, and soda. Knowing she didn't need the caffeine but would need the sugar, he grabbed a can of soda.

Lilah's eyes were closed as he approached. "We need to straighten it. You're going to have to pull it straight."

Isaac pressed the can into her hand. "I want you to take this."

Lilah opened her eyes and saw the pill in his hand. "Is that what I think it is?"

"Yeah. Trenton packed them."

Grimacing, she took it and swallowed it. "These things will chew a hole in your gut. Let's do this."

By the time he was done straightening her leg as best he could, she was silently crying. He felt tears sting his own eyes. He'd do anything to take the hurt from her. Quickly he tied the plastic to her leg with strips from one of his undershirts. She was starting to shiver and knew her body was going into shock. He took his coat that he'd tossed earlier and laid it over her legs. Her coat was probably as warm as his, so it would have to do to cover her torso. He rummaged through his suitcase for layers.

The sun was starting to set, and it went from gloomy to dark in the blink of an eye. "I don't want to leave you alone. But tomorrow I'll need to try to get a signal and get you out of here."

Lilah's head wobbled to the side. "Too dangerous at night, anyway. But Nash is expecting us back tonight."

He was counting on it. He had no idea how far he might have to trek to get cell reception. He'd camped enough in this area to know it was spotty at best. Enclosed, as they now were inside the SUV, he watched as snow fell. For now, they had food and water. When they didn't come back, Nash would call Gideon. And Gideon would call everyone he knew between here and D.C. to find them.

Isaac managed to wrap himself around Delilah without jarring her leg. He was glad the pain pill was kicking in and she was drowsy. She laid her head on his shoulder with her hand holding his as she dozed off. His body was stiffening up from the jarring fall. His left knee ached, and his chest and shoulder hurt from where the seat belt had cinched. But all in all, he was fine.

While Delilah dozed, he checked the wound on her head. It wasn't as bad as it had seemed. He took the opportunity to clean the wound and bandage it as much as her hair would allow. He then slouched down until he was lying beside her. He had the Glock 19 at hand should anyone come back.

* * *

Lilah woke with a full bladder. Isaac was behind her, his arms wrapped around her. She could hear his soft snoring in her ear. The back of her head hurt, and her leg and ankle were throbbing. The rest of her was sore and stiff. No doubt Isaac felt much the same. She was so thankful he wasn't hurt. Had the situation been reversed, there was no way she could have gotten him into the back of the SUV.

She took a moment to take stock of their situation. She could see sunlight through the snow-covered windows, but she would bet it was barely over the horizon. She could also see it had snowed more than a little while they'd slept. But right now, she was trying to figure out how in the world she was going to go to the bathroom.

Isaac stirred beside her as she shifted uncomfortably. She watched as his eyes opened.

Her voice sounded rusty when she spoke. "Good morning."

He stretched slightly beside her. "Morning."

She could feel her cheeks heating, but she had no choice. "I really have to go to the bathroom."

He sat up. "Same."

She snapped at him. "That's a lot easier for you than for me, you know."

He sat up and grabbed his broken glasses. "Hold on."

He climbed out of the side door and looked around. "We've got two choices: I can carry you and hold you while you go, or I can find something for you to use."

Just the thought of him holding her while she peed filled her with horrible embarrassment. "Option two."

He nodded and closed the door behind him.

Lilah shivered under her coat. Without his body heat beside her, the SUV felt very cold.

"There was nothing else I could think of."

She gaped at him when he handed her an empty plastic bag and the lid to the cooler. She took them.

"Just knock on the window when you're done."

It took a bit of ingenuity and inevitable pain in her leg, but she managed.

When she knocked and he came back to take the bag, he said nothing about the crimson color on her cheeks.

Lilah laid back. She watched him when he came back and crawled in beside her. "So now what?"

"I need to try to get a cell signal. You need more help than I can give you."

Lilah closed her eyes and struggled not to cry. "It's going to need surgery, isn't it?"

Isaac maneuvered and pulled her upper body against his chest. "I'm not a doctor."

She found she could laugh at that. "Well, you are, but I'll let that slide. I never told you why I limp. It's funny because I said the same thing to Nash after dinner with my mom and Rob, but I didn't really tell him. I was born with one leg shorter than the other. I had a few procedures done. It didn't go quite as planned."

"I assumed you had an accident or something."

Lilah shifted, trying to get comfortable. "No. The difference in length was enough to have to fix it surgically. It's awful what they do to fix it. They cut the bone and stretch your leg so that the bone grows together longer than it was. And when that wasn't good enough, I had to have the other leg shortened. They cut a piece out. I think this hurts worse."

Isaac shifted until he could grab the bottle of pain pills. He handed her one.

"Before I take this, I have a couple of questions for you."

Isaac sat up. "You deserve some answers."

"Do you know how to use that gun you've got tucked under your clothes? And who were the people who tried to kill us?"

"I know how to use the gun. And I know who tried to kill me. You were collateral damage."

Frustrated, she sat up on her elbows. "Words, Isaac. You usually have a bunch."

Isaac gazed at the snow-covered window. "Her name is Avery. Not sure what surname she might be using these days. I knew her as Major Avery Whitlock. We worked together at the Pentagon."

Lilah couldn't believe what she'd heard. "What? When did you work at the Pentagon?"

Isaac smiled at her incredulous tone. "Seems forever ago. I was twenty-one. I had gotten recruited through the university. A man approached me about doing some work for a special assignment. I was assigned to an undercover, stateside operation being run out of the Pentagon. Major Whitlock was in charge. No one knew why I was there, but I had been brought in to crack a code to find out who was selling sensitive information to a hostile country."

Lilah knew exactly where this was going. "And it was Avery."

He nodded. "It was Avery. She disappeared before she

could be arrested. She knew I was the one that turned her in. She had seduced one of the officers assigned to my team. He told her everything, right before she killed him. But she didn't know my real identity. She only knew me by an alias. After the national press published my face all over the news, I've been waiting for her to find me. My superior, a man named Monroe, said there was no way she was going to find me. That she was long gone. But he didn't know her like I did. I spent over a year tracking her and her movements after I got out, but I couldn't find her. After the attack, and six months passed, I thought I had gotten lucky. When our room was robbed, I made another call. He assured me she hadn't set foot on American soil since she'd run, or he would know about it."

Lilah felt sick to her stomach. "Could she have hired someone?"

He hesitated, then shook his head. "No, I don't think so. She was very hands on. She killed that kid herself without a second thought. No one would look at her and think she was a threat."

"Could it have been her at the hotel? The woman I met?"

"Too young. Avery is a good fifteen years older than me."

Lilah absorbed what he's said. "I can't believe it. You always seem, I don't know, not the type."

Isaac rubbed his temple. "You mean too studious and boring to have been involved in something like that. I was in for less than two years, but I learned a lot. One of them is how to protect myself. And my family. I was relieved when I got to take my name back and got the full-time assistant professor job at the university."

The more Lilah thought about it, the more sense it made. He might prefer teaching and writing, but he could have done anything with that brain of his. She could picture a twenty-one-year-old Isaac. Young, athletic, super smart. He would have been an ideal candidate for a mission like that.

Isaac pulled away. "Let's get some food in you before I go."

The sun was mostly up by the time they had eaten some of the snacks Trenton packed. He'd insisted she drink the bottle of water and helped with the bathroom situation one last time before he left. But before he took off, he'd kissed her. Hard. His vibrant blue eye had been intense, and then he'd turned and left without another word.

It was cold and she was tired. The pain pill she'd taken made her drowsy, but sleep eluded her. It felt like the temperature was dropping, and she was worried about Isaac. He'd brushed the snow off the back of the SUV so she could get some sunlight and look out the window. She could see how far they had slid down the hill before coming to a stop. No doubt the climb back up the hill hadn't been an easy one. She knew Isaac was fit, and that he'd have an easier time than she would making the trek, but she had to stop herself from imagining him falling as he made his way up.

It felt like hours before he came back. She cried a little in relief when he came back with a couple of local police officers and a small rescue team. The SUV was a wash, and because of where it was, the vehicle probably wouldn't be able to be towed until the ground fully froze, if even then. One of the officers had taken pictures and paint samples. In the end, she had to be carried out on a stretcher. An ambulance waited at the nearest accessible section of road from where they had gone off.

Isaac rode in the back of the ambulance with her and held her hand until she was wheeled into surgery.

Chapter Six

Isaac sat in the hospital room while Delilah slept. Nash would be there within the hour. Gideon had wanted to come, but Penny was still feeling ill, so he hadn't wanted to leave her. Trenton had come down with what Ginny and Gwenny had.

Isaac had waited anxiously while Delilah had been in surgery. Her ankle was broken, as were both her tibia and fibula. The doctor had been impressed with the makeshift splint, but Isaac was happy she was now in a proper cast. It was her right leg, so she wasn't going to be able to drive. He wasn't sure she realized it yet. She'd been too focused on the pain. But once she woke up and realized she couldn't drive, she was going to be frantic. As her mother's sole caretaker, this was another obstacle that had found its way into her life.

There was a light tap on the door, and Nash poked his head in. He came in and embraced his friend in a bear hug, then gave him a once over. "At least you're in one piece. How is she?"

Isaac led him to the hallway so they could chat. "Broken leg and broken ankle. The surgery went well, and the doctor said it would heal fine. The cut on the back of her head didn't need stitches; they just put a little glue on the cut. I learned Delilah is quite vain when it comes to her hair. She threatened the doctor when he wanted to shave around the wound."

That made Nash laugh, as Isaac had hoped. But then Nash was once again serious. "You were vague about what happened. You want to try the truth this time?"

Isaac had never told his friends about his time at the Pentagon. Delilah was the only person besides those he'd worked with who knew. He'd told the quartet he was going to work at a museum in London and work on a new book. It hadn't been a total lie. He'd eventually gone. And he'd written the book while on assignment. He had needed the calm environment to recuperate. Avery had managed to lodge a bullet in his shoulder blade. It had been a small caliber, and there had been no permanent damage. The familiarity of being surrounded by history had been exactly what he needed to recenter himself before he came home. When he had come home, his friends had embraced him, and life went back to normal.

"I should probably tell you with Trenton and Gideon on the phone. You're not going to like this."

Nash swore. "Like how I hadn't liked it when Clara kidnapped Penny and tried to kill her? Or how I hadn't liked it when you had chemicals tossed in your face, Trenton put himself in harm's way, and Lilah faced a crazed woman with a gun?"

Isaac scrubbed his hands over his face, a headache pounding behind his eyes. "Something like that."

Nash cursed again. "Now. Let's go. I don't think I can take any more of this."

Isaac glanced back into the room where Delilah was still sleeping. She hadn't stirred. He followed Nash outside. Nash dialed in the group. "All right, spill it, Isaac."

Isaac told the story much as he'd told it to Delilah. For her sake, he'd left out a few of the grisly details, but he told his friends the full truth, including watching a young man murdered and being shot in the shoulder. Gideon had gone silent, Trenton had exploded, and Nash, well, he couldn't tell what Nash was thinking.

Gideon interrupted Trenton's hollering. "All right. I'll talk to the local police in Vermont. And I'll see if Freya can help. She found Ginny's stalker. Maybe she can find this Avery Whitlock woman. The minute you get back to a computer, send me everything you know about her."

Isaac promised.

Nash hung up. His expression was still unreadable. "Hell, man, why didn't you tell us?"

"You know why. The three of you each lived through your own childhood hells. I just had a lousy father. At first, I was excited to join the operation. Young bravado, I guess. But things didn't turn out how I thought. A man died. Avery got away. Secrets were sold. It wasn't a successful mission. I just wanted to forget it ever happened. I went back to academia and my books."

Nash's hand fisted. "You knew that, given the opportunity, she'd come after you. And yet you let Ginny write that book."

Isaac turned his back on Nash and headed back inside to be with Delilah. He wanted to be there when she woke up. Nash kept pace beside him. "I'm not letting Ginny put in pictures. My publisher agreed to never show my face. The likelihood of someone recognizing me at a book signing or something like that was slim. And it has been almost fifteen years."

Isaac sighed with relief that Delilah was still sleeping.

Nash followed him inside. He kept his voice low. "You didn't have an affair with this Avery woman, did you?"

"No. She acted like she was interested in me, but there was something about her I didn't trust. She was at the top of my list. Because I ignored her flirting, she seduced the kid whom I worked with instead."

Nash chuckled. "You never were one who let your hormones control your decision making. Us mere mortals aren't so lucky. So, anything happen between you and Lilah?"

"You're really pushing your luck."

Nash let out a disgusted breath. "Figures. I set you up with the woman you've been mooning over for a year, and you don't take advantage. You know, if you keep it up, some other man is going to snatch her up."

Isaac turned on his friend. "Like you, perhaps?"

Nash held up both palms in surrender. "No, not me. Her mother took one look at me and knew I wasn't the man for her daughter. I told her you were. She agreed."

Isaac was now confused. "When did you meet Delilah's mother?"

Nash sat back in his seat. "Dinner. I met her mother and her mother's new boyfriend. Lilah was nervous about meeting him. As far as she knows, her mother hasn't dated since her father died. But her mom met this guy at the hospital when they were both having some tests done. Anyway, Lilah didn't want to face the situation alone, so she asked me to come. So I flirted a bit, charmed her mother, and her mother declared I was not the one. Go figure."

Isaac saw Delilah stir but didn't wake. "There is a lot to hate about you sometimes. You knew I'd be jealous that Delilah asked you on a date. But you were playing chaperone."

Nash tucked his tongue into his cheek. "I did kiss her."

"Yeah, well, so did I."

Nash slapped his friend on the back. "I like Lilah, so I'm not sure I should congratulate you or feel sorry for her. Don't screw it up, Isaac. You overthink everything."

Isaac leaned forward and rested his elbows on his knees. "I do, don't I? I'm trying to go with the flow here, but I think I might have already messed up my approach."

"I guess as long as it wasn't your usual one. The one where you're bluntly honest. I keep telling you, women like romance. Simply telling a woman you find her attractive and then expecting her to either take it or leave it is not romantic."

Isaac groaned. "I know. That's what I mean. I already told her I find her attractive. And I'm afraid I didn't stop there."

That piqued Nash's interest. "Do tell."

A soft voice came from the bed. "Don't you dare."

Isaac surged to his feet. He came to stand by Delilah's bed. "How do you feel?"

"Mmm. Tired. How long have I been asleep?"

Isaac took her hand and rubbed the back of her fingers. "About four hours, I guess. You woke briefly after the surgery, but then you dozed off. The doctor said the best thing for you was to rest. You're worn down."

Lilah turned her head. "Hi, Nash. Telling tales?"

"Just little ones." Nash leaned over her and gave her a light kiss on the forehead. "You two had us worried when you didn't come home. If Trenton weren't sick, he'd have come for you himself."

Lilah turned her hand so she could hold Isaac's. "Any word yet from the police?"

Isaac took the nearby chair and sat, not releasing her hand. "Not yet. But Gideon is on it. He's reached out to Freya to see if she can help. He figures if she can find lost cult members, one ex-military major should be easy."

Lilah's eyes narrowed. "You don't sound convincing."

Nash kicked Isaac's chair, and he stopped what he was going to say. Instead Isaac settled for making excuses. "I'm just tired. We both are. Nash is going to hang out and drive us back when you're released."

Lilah felt tears clogging her throat. "What am I going to do about my mom?"

Knowing it was inevitable, but hoping the tears would have held out a little longer, Isaac leaned over her, taking both of her hands in his. "You and your mom are going to stay with me. Your mom can have the room in the back that was for the housekeeper when the house was built. And I'll drive her. I think I've proven to myself I can handle it."

Tears dripped down her cheeks. "We'd be dead if it weren't for you."

Nash came up behind them. He set his hands on Isaac's shoulders. "You both need some rest. Isaac, I'll stay here. You need a shower, a shave, and a nap. Not necessarily in that order. And for pity's sake, take a pill for that headache."

Isaac was torn, but he was running on fumes. And Nash was right about the headache. "All right." Isaac leaned in and kissed Delilah lightly before pulling away.

Nash handed him the keys to his car. "I already brought your things to the hotel. The front desk is expecting you."

With one last look at Delilah, he left.

* * *

When Lilah woke again, Nash was dozing in one of the reclining chairs. His head was in an awkward position, and no doubt he was going to have a crick in his neck when he woke. Isaac hadn't yet returned. The curtains were open, and the sun was setting, so she hoped he was getting some sleep.

Nash stirred but didn't wake. But Lilah wasn't thinking about Nash; she was thinking about Isaac. She remembered him promising to take care of her and her mother. And she remembered him kissing her softly on the lips before leaving. It had been such a sweet kiss. And she didn't know what she was going to do.

Looking at Nash, all Lilah could think was why couldn't she start falling for him instead? Nash was smart, but he was into things like art and computers. They had more in common than she did with Isaac. Lilah liked binge-watching television after a long week of work, and Isaac preferred his head in a book. So far, they didn't like the same music or books, not that Lilah spent a lot of time reading. Being dyslexic, she preferred audio books. When she mentioned listening to books, Isaac had looked horrified. On top of that, she loved watching sports, and he disliked them. The only thing they seemed to have in common was food, but only if he cooked it. She hated cooking, and he lived for it.

She never should have kissed Isaac, she thought. Some part of her had hoped he would be as analytical in that as he was in everything else. But despite his outward appearance and despite his personality, there was passion buried underneath the staid clothes, the almost military haircut, and polished loafers. And once she'd started thinking about him being attracted to her, she found herself more and more attracted to him.

Nash's sleep-roughened voice pulled her from her thoughts.

"You look like you're trying to find the meaning of life inside that head of yours. I take it you're thinking about Isaac."

She and Nash had gotten close over the past year, and maybe he'd have some insight into Isaac's mind. "Yeah. He told me on the drive to the hotel that he was attracted to me. He sort of just threw it out there, and then he said it was his problem, not mine, when I told him I had never thought about him like that."

Nash yawned and stretched. "And now you're thinking about him like that."

"Yes. But I don't get it. Why me?"

Nash considered her question. "Part of it would be physical. He's a guy and he can't help it if he finds you physically attractive. But outward looks are never Isaac's main focus when it comes to women. And to be frank, there haven't been a lot of them. A lot of people find him boring. Just like you do. He's not exciting; he actually does prefer staying at home and enjoying an evening in. What he really wants is stability. Part of your charm is your love for your mother. You worry about her, and you worry about your situation. But in the end, you love her and want to do what's best. You're not selfish, I suppose, is one way to look at it. You know how to give and take."

Lilah winced as she shifted in the bed. "Now you're making me sound boring. But while maybe he finds me physically attractive, I'm not as smart as he is. I can't discuss literature or have discussions with him in French."

Nash's mouth twisted into a grimace. "Sorry about Stefan. I'd have warned you, but he's just something you have to experience on your own. But Isaac doesn't judge people on their intelligence. He'd probably kill me for telling you this, but all he ever wanted was to not be like his father."

Lilah tried to think if she had ever heard Isaac mention his father, or even his mother, but she couldn't recall. "He doesn't talk about them much, does he?"

"Dr. Theodore Brandt is an ass. It's as simple as that. He doesn't care or love anyone. Probably not even himself. The man is brilliant, and he thinks pretty much everyone else is beneath him. That includes his wife and only child. Isaac's mother, Millicent, is smart. But she is more artistic. She loves music and art. His father loves language, history, and politics. Isaac gets his writing talent from his mother, not his father. To this day, it ticks Senior off that his son's books are more popular than his own. I won't repeat what he thinks of his fiction. Isaac spent his childhood doing everything opposite of his father. But Isaac really does love language and history. He loves literature and art."

Lilah smiled to herself. She had watched Isaac these past few days spend his evenings reading. She could see peace and contentment while holding the old book and reading the words.

Nash continued. "Anyway, Isaac was very young when he decided he didn't want to be his father. He learned to cook, garden, and even clean. His father swore he would disown him. Practically did, if you want the truth. His mother, too, because she bends to her husband's will in all things. But Isaac eventually determined it wasn't the books or the writing or his father's career that were the problem. It was the man himself. So Isaac started embracing a lot of the things his father did, but that made things with his father worse. His father sees him as a rival. I think Isaac was twelve when he vowed to put his father in his place. Isaac has more degrees, more books, more money, speaks and reads more languages, and has more accolades than his father could ever hope to have. But what Isaac learned the most was that you shouldn't judge or look down on others. That's all his father ever did to him and to everyone his father knows."

Lilah thought about what it must have been like growing up with a man like his father, one you could never please and one with whom you could never find common ground. How terrible Isaac must have felt, knowing his father saw him as a rival, not as a son whom he should love and support. Her parents loved her and supported her every day of their lives. It hurt her to know that Isaac hadn't been loved like that.

But he had his friends. Friends who would drop everything, do anything, to be there for each other. "So how did all of you become friends? You all seem so different. I sort of know how you and Gideon became friends."

Nash tipped his head up as he thought about the past. "Isaac. We met through our parents. My father was getting involved in politics back then when I was around ten. Dr. Brandt had come to one of my father's fundraisers. Dad knew just about everyone in those days. Isaac's father was a diplomat, but he hadn't had an assignment in a while. Most people simply didn't want to work with him. Anyway, he came and dragged Isaac with him. My guess is that he only came so he could schmooze some influential people in D.C. I found out later the only reason he brought Isaac was to show Isaac how much better he was than my dad, who had business acumen but hadn't finished college. Anyway, I was bored, and Isaac looked my age. So I asked him if he wanted to go play with my toys. Isaac shrugged and pushed his glasses further up his nose, but he followed me."

Nash turned his eyes to her. "Poor kid didn't have toys at his house. So I showed him my collection of action figures, gave him a few to take home, and we became friends. We started hanging out at school together. We didn't get close until after what happened with my grandfather. I was pretty messed up. Gideon started coming to the school and joined us. So there we were, the three of us. I was messed up and wasn't coping well, and Gideon was a fish out of water. Isaac brought a sense of reason. He found ways to pull both of us back from the brink of our personal demons. Isaac then became a tutor, and that's how he met Trenton. Trenton was far behind, academically speaking, when he came to the school. The cult he grew up in wasn't big on formal education. Isaac brought Trenton into the group. We just clicked. When we were together, we could be who we really were, we could share our secrets, and we could simply have fun."

Lilah wiped away stray tears. "It's rare, your friendship. I hope the four of you know that. I've probably told you more of my secrets than I have to any other person in my entire life."

Nash laughed. "I make a great girlfriend."

Lilah smiled, but she was serious. "You probably are the best girlfriend I've ever had. I was thinking life would be so much easier if I were attracted to you instead of Isaac. We have a lot more in common than Isaac and I do. But you didn't make my toes curl when you kissed me."

Nash put a hand across his heart. "You wound me, Lilah. I may never recover. But now I know for sure Isaac made a move. He refused to kiss and tell. Wouldn't even admit he had. I had to trick him into admitting he'd kissed you, but he was short on details."

Lilah closed her eyes, thinking about the kiss. "I kissed him first. He kept saying his attraction wasn't my problem. But I disagreed. So I thought that if I kissed him, I wouldn't like it, and I could forget about it."

"But you got curling toes instead. Nice."

Lilah made a humming sound. "No one has ever curled my toes before. But I think it would be better to stay away.

He needs someone more like him."

Nash disagreed. "You are exactly what he needs. Trust me. He doesn't need someone just like him. They'd bore each other to death. He needs someone who can love him, and not for his mind. Someone who can make him laugh, make him angry, and my dear, he was so beside himself after I told him I was taking you on a date; he couldn't contain his jealousy. I swear he was ready to punch me."

"He was pretty mad at me, too. You think that's a good thing, huh?"

Nash rose and stretched. "Definitely. You're my friend, Lilah, but Isaac is my brother. I don't think he's ever really known happiness in a relationship, outside of the ones with the quartet. So I'm not asking you to fall in love with him. I'm not asking you to devote yourself to him. I just want you to think about him, not as a genius, but as a normal man. All I'm asking is that you give him a chance. You might be surprised."

Lilah promised. "I will. Are you leaving?"

"Yeah. I'm going to check on Isaac. I thought he'd be back here by now. Hopefully your doctor discharges you tomorrow, and then we'll figure out the next step of our plan. Isaac told us about his time working at the Pentagon and who he thinks ran you two off the road. I must tell you, Lilah, that worries me. He never breathed a word."

Lilah shivered and tugged the blanket around her neck. Nash kissed her on the cheek and took his leave. She couldn't believe Isaac had kept a secret like that from his friends. With all that the men had been through together, she couldn't believe he had kept this from them. She wasn't sure what that meant, but she had a feeling that in Isaac's life, anything he kept secret must have been pretty bad.

Chapter Seven

Isaac and Nash were fighting. Lilah sat on the sidelines, watching with wide eyes. Isaac had come to the conclusion that he needed to disappear for a while. Nash told him what he thought of that idea, using some pretty salty language. Isaac tried reasoning with Nash, and when that failed, he was reduced to yelling. It was sort of fascinating to watch Isaac lose his temper, at least when it wasn't aimed at her.

"I'm not putting everyone in danger. Just look what happened." Isaac pointed a finger Lilah's way.

Lilah looked at her cast. Yes, her leg complicated things. So many things.

Nash retaliated. "And you're even dumber than you look if you think your friends are going to abandon you while some psycho woman is trying to kill you. We stick together; you got that?"

Lilah figured Nash had a point. Since she'd known them, Cantwell's office had been burned down, Nash's sister Penny kidnapped by their cousin Clara, who was then shot and killed by Gideon, Trenton hunted by a crazed cult member, his now-wife Ginny terrorized by the crazed cult member's son, and Lilah held at gunpoint by said crazed cult member. Now she had her leg and ankle broken after having been run off the road into a ravine by an ex-major who wanted to kill Isaac. If she had any common sense, she'd make a run for it. But her normal supply of common sense and self-preservation seemed to be in short supply.

Right now, all she wanted to do was fling herself at Isaac and kiss him. Maybe drag him into this bed with her. And that wasn't the craziest thing. She'd gone from zero to a hundred in her feelings for Isaac in less than a week.

"I have to leave. My old boss has made it clear that he won't protect me. All he keeps saying is that it wasn't Avery. But I know it was. It can't be anyone else. So now I need to hunt her down and find her. And I'm not risking anyone else."

Nash poked him in the chest. "Gideon already has Freya on it. All you have to do is go hole up somewhere until Freya finds her."

Isaac smacked Nash's hand. "Such faith. You don't even know the woman. So what if Freya found Trenton's cultist? Delilah's friends found her first."

That wasn't quite how it went, but Lilah wasn't going to argue the point. "Can I interrupt?"

Both men turned angry eyes her way: one pair of gray and one blue. She held up a placating hand. "First, Isaac, you promised me you would help me with my mom. You can't do that if you disappear. Second, Nash, you should understand better than anyone the desire to protect those you love. That's what Isaac thinks he's doing. Third, Isaac, you really are dumber than you look if you think your three best friends are going to sit on the sidelines while this woman hunts you down. I have met Freya, and trust me, she's going to be your greatest asset. And this way, with Gideon in the loop, none of you will do anything too stupid. You can't go all vigilante on this Avery woman. Get proof, then take it to your so-called friend. He won't have a choice but to deal with her."

Nash's eyes danced. "Man, you're sexy when you're mad."

Isaac glared at Nash. "Don't make me punch you."

Lilah felt the thrill of his words straight through her. But she needed to focus. "My mother is going to be gone for another week. I say Isaac and I lay low. We have to assume Avery, or whoever broke into our hotel room, knows who I am. Isaac, you say you love camping. We can go hide in the woods somewhere while Freya digs. And then we'll worry about the next step. I can't leave my mom alone once she's back. And I'm sorry, but it freaks me out a little that she might decide to shack up with her boyfriend permanently if I'm not around. I'm having enough of a hard time with this romantic getaway."

Isaac's eyes narrowed in thought. "Actually, it's a good idea. If your mom stays with Robert, then I won't have to worry about you accidentally getting your mother involved. You should call her and ask her to stay with him while we sort this out."

Lilah gaped. "That's not what I said."

Isaac glanced at Nash. "All right. Delilah and I lay low. Delilah's mom shacks up with her boyfriend. You go back and work with Gideon and Freya. We can use our old secret email to keep in touch."

Nash agreed. "It's a plan. Lilah, go call your mother. Give her as few details as you can. Just tell her you've fallen madly in love with Isaac and you're running off together for a while."

Lilah snorted very unladylike. "My mother will never

believe I've run off. Fallen madly in love, maybe, but not running off."

Nash shrugged. "Crazier things have happened. Go call her while Isaac and I find a place to stash you."

Lilah wasn't sure how she'd lost that argument. But she went and did as she was asked. Her mother seemed delighted by the situation.

Priscilla's pleased tone came over the line. "I knew Nash was not the one. This Isaac is. I'm so glad you two are hitting it off so well. I want to see my grandchildren before I die."

Lilah sputtered. "You're not going to die anytime soon. And don't start planning a wedding yet, okay? You and Rob seem to be having a great time. So if he wouldn't mind letting you stay with him. Just for a short while. I'm sure his place is nicer than our apartment, given that he's a doctor and all."

Lilah could hear Rob's voice in the background. Her mother started giggling, wished her good luck, and hung up. Lilah was torn between happiness for her mother and embarrassment because her mother was embroiled in a hot affair with a short and round retired cardiologist.

Isaac found her lying on the bed, her leg propped up on a stack of pillows. "So, is she going to stay with him?"

Lilah felt the bed dip where he came to sit beside her. "Yes. I think she's in love, Isaac. Him, too. I'm happy for her, but a little weirded out. And she seems thrilled at the prospect that I'm running off with you. She hasn't even met you."

"We can remedy that when we get back. Are you sure

you're up to this? I have a friend who has a cabin near here. We ski together when Nash can't make it. He says we can borrow it. But that means being secluded with me until we can find proof that Avery is the one who attacked us."

Lilah wet her dry lips. "I'm not afraid to be alone with you, if that's what you're asking. And maybe we can get to know each other better."

Isaac looked deep into her eyes. She wasn't sure what he saw there, but it seemed to satisfy him. "All right. Nash is going to go buy us a car, and then we can be on our way. We'll need to stop for supplies, but we should be settled into the cabin tonight."

* * *

It hadn't been until Lilah had been propped up in the back seat of a brand-new Land Rover that she realized Nash really had gone out and bought them a car. She didn't know anyone else except Nash who could toss around that kind of money without a second thought. Well, except maybe Trenton. The vehicle was decked out, and while she wasn't sure how much a vehicle like this cost, no doubt Nash hadn't blinked an eye as he'd paid for the vehicle in full. There were still times, times like now, when she wasn't sure what she had gotten herself into when she'd gone to work for Cantwell.

These four men were unlike any she'd ever known. Her dad had been a soft-spoken man who had gone through life seemingly satisfied with what life had given him. Her boyfriends when she was younger were mostly artists, musicians, or computer nerds like she was. It was hard to remember what they were like. A few different men had drifted in and out of her life, and she hadn't minded. Most were decent men, but none of them really stood out in her memory. It was a sad state for a thirty-one-year-old woman that none of her would-be suitors were memorable. And it had been so long since she'd been on a date, unless you counted Nash, and she didn't, that she didn't know if she had a type anymore. She always thought she'd eventually end up with a man like her dad: steady as a rock, always there for her, soft-spoken, and supportive.

Isaac, well, she thought of him as soft-spoken like her dad, unless he was arguing with Trenton. Trenton had a knack for pushing Isaac's buttons. It seemed Nash did, too. It was only in the past week that Lilah had seen a different side to him. But Isaac was analytical. Her dad had relied more on his gut instincts and made snap decisions more than he'd ever been contemplative. Isaac could drive one nuts while coming to a decision.

But when they'd been forced off the road, he had done what needed to be done, formed a plan, and executed it. She couldn't help but wonder if most of his plans went the way he planned them. And she couldn't help but wonder what his plan was with her. She figured he must have one, though he had seemed resigned to keeping his feelings and his hands to himself. She wondered if their kiss had thrown him off balance as much as it had her. It was a pleasant thought.

It was after midnight when Isaac pulled into a driveway that could barely be seen from the road. The Land Rover bounced half a mile over ruts and gravel before he pulled up to a darkened cabin.

Isaac kept the vehicle running while he climbed out. She turned and watched as he opened the hatch.

She yawned and shivered as the cold air hit her in the face. "Sorry, I'm not much help."

Isaac nodded at her, as if in agreement. It made her smile.

"Just stay there and I'll come get you. The cabin has electricity, but no furnace. We'll get settled in and I'll start a fire. I'll have you warmed up in no time."

Lilah waited as bitterly cold air blew. She watched Isaac make several trips. Nash had hooked them up with food and supplies. Thankfully they had all their clothes and personal belongings. She could only imagine the clothes Nash would pick out for her.

Isaac shut off the engine, slammed the door, and came around to the passenger side. He looked at her for a moment before holding out a hand. "Let's get you out of there. It's icy, so I don't want you walking."

Lilah took the hand he was offering, and he managed to slide her forward so that he could get his arm under her knees, and she could wrap her arms around his neck. He carried her inside like she weighed nothing.

The interior was spartan. There were two full-size beds against the back wall. Off to the left was what she assumed passed for a kitchen. There was a wood-burning stove, an oversized fridge, and scant counter space. To the right, there was a worn couch and a huge flat screen television. She had seen a satellite dish on the roof.

Isaac carried her to one of the beds and set her down. He then grabbed the crutches he had already brought in and put them where she could reach them. "Bathroom is through that door. There is a hot water tank; it doesn't last long, but you can get enough hot water for a quick shower or a shallow bath."

Lilah grabbed her duffle bag and rummaged for a nightgown. "I'm just glad there's plumbing."

Isaac shrugged. "Compost toilet, but it does the trick."

Lilah wrinkled her nose at that but didn't bother to complain. As long as there was hot water in her future, she could deal with a compost toilet.

Lilah looked around the small cabin again. "Somehow I can't imagine Nash here."

Isaac straightened from where he had been rummaging through his suitcase. "He loves fishing, and there are some good spots around here. But he complained about the cabin and the lack of amenities. A lot. But don't let him fool you. He spent months on an oil rig and shared barracks with a bunch of men."

Lilah's brows knitted at that. "An oil rig? When?"

Isaac pulled out a pair of sweatpants and a fresh t-shirt. "Twenty-two. It was while I was at the Pentagon. He said he needed to go away and burn off the anger that was building inside him. He had just lost Maggie and had so much pent-up rage in him. He needed a physical outlet. His mom panicked when he thought about joining the marines. When he read about the oil rigs needing workers, he jumped at it. I can't say he was fixed when he came back, but he managed to get his demons under control."

Lilah hugged her nightgown to her stomach. "I know his fiancée died. And I know his grandfather was murdered. But I can't help but feel there's more to it."

"Isn't there always." Isaac gestured toward the bathroom. "Why don't you use the bathroom first. It's late."

She curbed her curiosity, grabbed the crutches and her toiletry bag, and made her way to the bathroom. While she was grateful to have the crutches, she hated the fact that she was once again forced to use them. She grimaced when she looked in the mirror. Her hair was a tangled mess, and she had some serious dark circles under her eyes. Her sleep, which had been haunted by the memory of a crazy woman and a gun, was now mixed with dreams of falling over cliffs, except this time they didn't make it.

"Need help?"

"No, I'm fine." Lilah washed her face, brushed her teeth, managed to get the tangles out of her hair, and changed into her nightgown. The sleeveless nightgown fell past her knees, but she felt extremely exposed. But the only other option was sleeping in her clothes.

She felt Isaac's eyes on her as she made her way back to the bed. "All yours."

Isaac disappeared. Lilah was grateful the sheets were fresh and the blanket heavy. The fire Isaac had lit was warming the room, but the wind was blowing and howling outside the cabin walls.

Isaac came back out a few minutes later dressed in his sweats and t-shirt. He turned off the lamp, and the room was lit by the fire.

Lilah rolled onto her side so that she was facing Isaac,

and her broken leg was propped on top of the other. "So what else do you like to do besides reading, writing, cooking, teaching, and skiing?"

Isaac's covers rustled as he rolled so that he could see her. "What?"

Lilah tucked her arm to her chest. "Well, how can I get to know you if you don't tell me things about yourself?"

Isaac took off his glasses, another item courtesy of Nash, and set them on the table between the two beds. "Ah, like twenty-questions. I like going to museums. My favorite is the British Museum in London. Mostly I like London. I'll have to take you there one day."

Lilah yawned again. It didn't get past her notice that it was the second time he casually suggested future travel plans with her. "I've never traveled. Never had the time or the money. I bet London is nice. Do you have any other family besides your parents and the quartet?"

Isaac tucked an arm under his pillow and kept his eyes on her. "Not really. My mom is an only child. Her parents died when I was young. My dad never talked about his parents. He does have a brother, but he stays as far away from my dad as he can get. My uncle was the black sheep, from what I understand. Sex, drugs, and rock 'n' roll."

"I hardly see you drink more than a beer or a glass of wine. I'm guessing no drugs."

"No."

Lilah yawned again and felt her eyes start to droop. "Same, no drugs. I did date a musician once; he played guitar in an alternative rock band. I dropped him when I found out he had a drug problem."

Isaac rolled onto his back. "Let's pick this back up tomorrow."

Lilah murmured her agreement and fell asleep.

* * *

Isaac watched Delilah as she sat at the small dining table and ate her breakfast while she doodled on her sketch pad. She hated it when he watched her while she worked, but he couldn't seem to keep his eyes off her. She had her damp hair plaited down her back, her broken leg propped up on a chair, and was wearing her normal clothes. There wasn't anything about her today that was different from any other day. But something felt different.

He'd half expected her to pick up where she'd left off last night. He'd been thinking about it most of the morning. She hadn't asked him about his parents. Isaac picked up his coffee and joined her. "What did Nash tell you about my parents?"

She absently answered. "That your dad is an ass."

Isaac laughed. "That really does sum him up. He likes to think he's a complicated man, but at the end of the day, an ass is really all he is."

Lilah set her pencil down. "I think my dad would have liked you. He was smart, though not like you. He was valedictorian of his high school. He didn't go to college, but he loved to read. History and politics, mostly. History fascinated him. He read some of your books. It wasn't until a couple of months after we met that I remembered. Gideon was reading one of them, and I recognized the cover. I took a look at my father's bookcases and found three of them."

Isaac was flattered. "Did you read them?"

Lilah bit her lip. "Maybe."

Isaac took pity on her and grabbed her coffee mug so he could refill it. "I'll take that as a no. You said he also liked politics?"

Lilah thanked him as he handed her the cup. "He never picked political sides, but he kept up on current events and the state of our government. He said D.C. was like no other place he'd ever lived. He'd traveled a lot before he met my mom. He was an army brat, and he just kept on going until he met her. He never traveled again. I was born not long after they got married, and life got in the way."

"Doesn't it always? So what else do you want to know about me?"

Lilah tipped her head and her eyes narrowed. "In a hurry to answer my questions?"

Isaac rose and went to the window. "I'd like to know how I'm shaping up in your mind."

The room was quiet for a time. Then he felt Delilah's hand on his shoulder. "It's not like you have to pass some test, Isaac."

Isaac turned to face her. "Don't I? In the end, either I pass the test, or I fail it. If I pass it, then you decide if you want me or not. If I fail, then we're done."

Lilah set her crutches against the counter, wrapped her arms around his waist, and leaned her head against his chest.

Isaac closed his eyes for a moment and savored the feel

of her against his chest. His arms closed around her. "I'm sorry. I'm pushing you, and I don't mean to."

Lilah pulled away. "Okay. Next question. I heard you tell Trenton that you want to get married, have children, have grandchildren, and grow old with the mother of those children. Did you mean that?"

Nothing like putting a man on the spot. Isaac cleared his throat. "I had a feeling you overheard that. Trenton liked to play into his playboy image before he met Ginny. Nash, too, but he swears he's never getting married. Gideon was too focused on work to have much time for relationships. And Penny was the only woman he had eyes for. In a way, I think I'm more like Gideon, except I didn't have a specific woman in mind. But I had an idea of who she would be. And in that perfect world, yes, we would marry, have a family, and grow old together."

Lilah bit the side of her lip, but then asked, "Do I fit the idea of that woman?"

Isaac took her arm, hoping she wouldn't pull away when he answered her. "No."

Lilah tried to free her hand, but he kept hold of her wrist. "Jeez, Isaac, you need to learn to lie."

Isaac used his grip to pull her closer. "I don't need to. I couldn't have imagined you if I tried. You're more than I thought I wanted. And to answer the question that I think you were asking, I want you to be that woman. You just have to decide if I can be the man for you."

Isaac saw her hesitation, but he understood it. He was so much further ahead than she was. Now he had to wait to see if she wanted to catch up or run. But he wasn't so noble that he wasn't willing to help her along. He pulled her even closer and wrapped his arms around her waist, letting her steady herself against him.

He bent his head to her and brushed his lips across hers. He kept the caresses light, not devouring her like he had the last time. He simply wanted to enjoy her, to savor. Sunlight poured over them as he brought her closer, cupping her cheek in one hand as he continued to kiss her. She was so sweet, and he wanted her more than he had words to describe. With one last soft caress, he lifted his head and released her until she was balanced on her good leg.

He couldn't tell what she was thinking. So he helped her back to the chair and grabbed his laptop so they could work. Because if he didn't occupy his mind and his hands, he might find himself pushing her for more than she was ready for.

Lilah opened her laptop. They worked in silence for a time. Then Lilah let out a deep breath. "Here."

Isaac slid her laptop so he could read it when she pushed it his way. "You're done?"

"No. But I'm going to let you see what I've done so far. The art is done for the first five chapters. Stefan liked them even though they needed some work. Hopefully you like them."

Isaac wasn't surprised by the quality of the work. Delilah had proven time and again that she was a master of her craft. But these were beyond what he had expected. The first half of the novel introduced the reader to the world of Cantwell. In the war-torn land, there was still so much beauty to be found. She had gone with vivid colors not unlike the game itself. But there was depth to these, deeper shading and shadows that drew the reader in.

"You never cease to amaze me."

Lilah let out the breath she'd been holding. "Nash wanted something darker to contrast the game. I just couldn't. That's why I've been keeping them secret until I had more chapters done. The game is so vivid and full of color and emotion."

"I'm not worried about Nash. When he sees these, he'll be counting dollars."

Lilah laid a hand over his. "You really do like them?"

Isaac gave her his full attention. "You say I paint pictures with words. But I can't do this. I can't take words and make them seen. And remember, my name is on this, too. Trust me, if I didn't like them, I'd say so."

Lilah took her laptop back. "If you could visit anywhere, where would you go?"

Isaac kept his laptop where it was. They were back to twenty questions. The way he saw it, as long as she kept asking, he was still in the running. He pointed at her laptop. "Cantwell."

She gave him a huge smile and went back to work.

Chapter Eight

"Aren't you bored yet?" Lilah flipped off the television. They had been in the cabin for two days. And while they had both gotten a lot of work done on the graphic novel, the evenings were getting more difficult. Isaac seemed perfectly content to sit by the fire and read. She couldn't help but feel that he spent a lot of nights like this. Except he probably spent most of them alone. As far as she knew, he hadn't had a girlfriend in the year she'd known him. And if the guys were around, there would be food, beer, and lots of conversation.

When they weren't working, mostly she thought about Isaac. She was still sorting out her feelings. She found she enjoyed talking to him. She could forget he was a genius and just chat with him like she would with the other guys. But there was a new layer forming. He hadn't kissed her again after their first morning here. She could feel his eyes on her, but he seemed to be giving her the space and time she needed. She'd definitely asked him more than twenty questions in the past two days.

But what about her feelings? Since they met, she had been keeping him away, keeping any relationship, even friendship, from forming behind a wall of animosity. She wasn't a fan of self-reflection, but she was starting to wonder if the wall was a form of self-preservation. She didn't think a man like him would be attracted to her. But if his watchful eyes and tantalizing kisses were any indication, he was attracted. And if she said the word "yes," he would act on it.

Part of her, the part that longed and wished for a husband and family, knew she couldn't find a better man than Isaac. He was reliable, loyal, trustworthy, and compassionate. And he would never abandon his family. He would stand by her no matter what. There would be affection and caring. There would be love and passion. But she would never have those things if she didn't make the next move. He seemed to be waiting for her to decide.

Was she attracted? Oh, yes. Behind the glasses and precision-cut hair, and underneath the scholarly clothes and soft timbre of his voice, the man was ridiculously attractive. He was tall, which she liked. He had broad shoulders and an expanse of chest that she wanted to drape herself over. He was athletic, and his body looked it. The longer they were together, the more they talked, worked, and got to know each other, the more she was starting to want.

She watched with narrowed eyes as he stretched in response to her interruption.

Isaac rubbed his eyes beneath his glasses. "No. But my eyes are getting tired. Tomorrow we should take a break from work."

Lilah lifted her broken leg up off the couch. "And do what?"

Isaac set the book aside. "That's a loaded question. If we had a sled, I could pull you behind me while we got some fresh air."

"We might have to settle for the porch. Unless you want to turn your suitcase into a sled. It's been pretty handy so far."

Isaac chuckled. "That it has. We could also go for a drive. Maybe get dinner out. Or we could get more supplies we don't need, or maybe some books that are more your style."

Lilah pointed at her tablet lying on the bed. "That's what that is for."

Isaac shook his head. "Not the same."

Lilah shrugged. "You know, we don't have a lot in common outside of work."

Isaac gave the remark serious thought. "Do you like animals?"

Lilah wasn't sure where he was going with this, but she answered. "Sure, who doesn't? But neither of us has pets."

Isaac raised his hand and held up two fingers. "Do you like kids?"

Lilah nodded. "I do. I'd like to have some one day. But neither of us has them yet."

Isaac raised a third finger. "Do you like road trips?"

Lilah laughed. "Yes, I do. When my company is not being cranky."

Isaac gave her a nod. "So we're at three things in common. I'm sure we can come up with some more."

Lilah held up a finger. "I like to eat your food. So we both like food."

Isaac's eyes darkened and ticked up two more fingers. "I enjoyed kissing you. Did you enjoy kissing me?"

Lilah felt heat gathering in her belly. "Yes."

Isaac dropped his hand. "So five. We can find five more tomorrow."

Lilah watched in disbelief as he left and went to the bathroom. She had sworn he was going to come to her and kiss her. Trust Isaac to not do the normal thing. The man needed a woman to loosen him up. Maybe bring out a more playful side. The sudden desire to be that woman was like a lightning strike. And she understood exactly what Nash had meant when he told her Isaac needed a woman like her. In the quiet of the room, Lilah spoke out loud. "Well, who would have thought I'd find myself falling in love with Dr. Isaac Brandt?"

Isaac's voice came through the bathroom door. "Did you say something?"

Lilah lied. "No."

Isaac came out a little while later. "Want some help getting a bath ready?"

Lilah perked up at that. "Yes, please."

Lilah waited while he ran the bath water, gathered her things, and took them to the bathroom for her. He had helped her yesterday morning. He had even washed her hair for her. Her leg had hurt something awful afterward, but it had been amazing to have clean hair again.

Lilah used her crutches to pull out a fresh nightgown and wrapped up her hair. She came in as he was shutting off the water. "All ready?"

Isaac set out a towel and washrag for her. "Holler if you need me."

Lilah waited until he shut the door. She then managed to strip and get into the tub. The room had a lamp instead of an overhead light, and she found herself relaxing in the warm water. She tried to shut off her brain, but all she could do was think about Isaac in the other room. His hair had been damp, and he'd taken time to shave. She was starting to like the masculine stubble; it gave him a rough edge to his looks. On the other hand, she was used to the very proper Dr. Brandt, and the proper Dr. Brandt was always perfectly groomed.

She closed her eyes and thought about how it would feel to have the very proper Dr. Brandt make love to her. Would he take his time, or would he rush through it? Would he kiss her like he had that first time, out of control and wanting her?

They'd only been together a little over a week. But a lot had happened. She had been signed to a three-book deal with a real agent who was going to get her and Isaac's novels published. She had almost been killed. Again. Her mom had a new boyfriend. She had surgery. And she had learned more about Isaac in the past two days than she had in the past year.

She shifted in the tub, and the water caressed her breasts. What would it feel like to have his hands on her? What would it feel like to have his body gliding over hers?

Lilah opened her eyes. "Damn."

With some effort and some slight muscle strain, she got herself out of the tub. She dried off and pulled her nightgown over her head. She went to the mirror and released her hair. She fluffed it over her shoulders. She then looked herself in the eyes. They were darkened with desire. Desire for Isaac. "I think I'm losing my mind."

Lilah finished her nighttime routine. Grabbing her crutches, she made her way out of the bathroom. She found

Isaac sitting by the fire. The flames' reflections danced on his golden skin.

She came to him. "Help me sit?"

Isaac stood and grabbed the blanket from his bed. He tossed it on the floor and helped ease her down. "Feel better?"

Lilah stretched out her bare legs, suddenly wishing she'd taken the time to shave them. "Yes. But I think you can make me feel even better."

Isaac's eyes narrowed on her. "How?"

Lilah patted the spot next to her. "First, you sit."

Isaac obeyed. "And?"

Lilah scooted closer. "Now, you kiss me."

Isaac hesitated. But then he brought his mouth to hers. She nibbled at his lips as she brought her hand up to feel the smoothness of his jaw. He returned the kiss but pulled away when she tried to get closer.

Lilah, feeling emboldened, managed to get to her knees despite the cast and brought one of her legs between his and put a hand on his chest. "Now you make love to me."

"Don't play with me, Delilah."

Lilah shifted back so she could look into his eyes. "Who's playing?"

Isaac started to pull away, but she gripped his t-shirt so he wouldn't. "I've been thinking about you. For days now, I've done nothing but think about you. I think about you and me. You said you were attracted to me. You said you wanted to have sex with me. I've decided I'm attracted to you, and I want you the way you want me. I know it took me a little longer to get to this point than it did for you, but

I think I'm caught up."

Isaac brought his arms around her, his hands sliding over her hips. Isaac brought his lips to hers. "You have no idea how badly I want you, Delilah. But you need to be sure. I won't be able to let you go after this. We can't go back to being friends."

Lilah brought her other knee between his thighs. "I hope so, Isaac. I really do."

Isaac groaned and took her mouth with his. There was no hesitation, no tentative exploration. He devoured her. It came as a shock to her how tight a leash he'd kept himself on. Now that she had given him the words he wanted to hear, he let himself go.

He bit her lip, then soothed it. His teeth raked down the soft skin of her neck. His fingers were rough on her skin as he eased up her nightgown so he could touch her bare flesh. In seconds, he had her naked. She watched as he took in the sight of her bare breasts, took her wrists in his hands, and shifted their positions until she was on her back beneath him. He took a nipple into his mouth and sucked at her hard enough to have her arching off the blanket. She parted her legs for him so he could settle against her and wrapped her good leg around his waist. In return, he gave her other breast the same attention.

Desire, unlike any she'd known, took over. Now she was as frantic to have him as he was for her. She ran her hands over his chest under his t-shirt and struggled to get a grip on the fabric so she could get it off. Instead, he sat back on his knees so he could pull his shirt off and toss it. He tugged her up so that she was sitting with her legs still wrapped around him, his arms supporting her around her back. Her breasts were crushed against his chest, and she wriggled against him, needing the friction of skin against skin.

He took her mouth once again while she tried to get to the waistband of his sweats. They were tied, and she couldn't seem to get them undone. She could feel his erection eagerly pressing against the fabric. Distracted, she cupped him through the fabric. He arched his hips to press himself more firmly against her. She measured the length of him.

He pressed her hands harder against him while managing to untie his pants while she still cradled him. Moaning, Isaac eased her back down on the floor, forcing her to release him, and stood. He grabbed the waistband of his sweats, but then he stopped.

She saw him release his hold on the fabric. "Isaac, I need you to hurry this up."

"Delilah, I don't have protection. With everything else going on in your life, I don't think you really want to add a baby to the mix."

Lilah gave him a very womanly smile. "Go look in the bottom of your duffle bag."

He hesitated for a moment, but then turned to rummage through the bag. He pulled out a small box. "Trenton."

"All of your friends are conspiring against you."

Isaac grabbed a condom from the box and stripped off the rest of his clothes. Lilah watched in fascination as he rolled the condom on.

Isaac came back down on his knees, kneeling between her thighs. His hand cupped her, much as she had him. He stroked her flesh, and she shivered in his arms. He came over her, his hips pressing into hers. He then stroked her again with his fingers, testing her readiness.

Lilah's hips reared as he stroked a finger inside her for the first time. "Isaac, now."

He looked into her eyes as he brought their bodies together. Their gazes held until he was fully inside her. His forehead dropped to hers, their bellies pressed together. Burying his face in her neck, he stayed where he was for a moment. He kissed everywhere he could reach: her neck, her chin, her eyes, and then her mouth. Only after he seemed satisfied kissing her did he pull slightly out of her, then slowly push back in. After a few measured strokes, his control broke. His pace quickly picked up; his hips surged against hers.

Lilah wrapped one thigh around his back and wrapped her arms around him so she could pull herself closer. As frantic as he was, her hips matched his rhythm. She could feel his breath on her cheek. She could hear the sound of skin sliding against skin. She could hear her own whimpers as she felt herself tightening around him, felt the pleasure crest of having him inside her, moving within her. Gasping for breath, she felt herself go over the edge. The last thing she heard was his harsh cry as he bit her neck and followed.

Afterward, she was aware of their breathing, almost in unison, and the sound of the crackling fire. She thought she might have passed out for a moment, but then she felt his lips kissing her neck where he'd lightly bitten her skin. She had this irrational hope that he had left his mark on her.

He lifted so that he could look down on her. "I'd ask if

you were okay, but you look pretty pleased right now."

Lilah pulled him back to her so she could kiss him. "I knew."

He returned the soft caress. "Knew what?"

"That there was passion in you. The first time I kissed you, I wanted it to be boring because I didn't think you and I could work. But it wasn't. You curled my toes. I knew right then and there that there would be fireworks if I let you make love to me. I was right."

Isaac pulled out of her and stood. He stripped off the condom and tossed it in the trash. Then he went to his duffle and pulled out another one. "Let's set off some more."

* * *

Sunlight was coming through the closed curtains when Isaac woke. The fire was nothing but smolders. He didn't know what time it was, and he didn't really care. Three times he'd made love to Delilah. He was trying to remember if there had ever been a woman like her in his life before. If there had ever been a woman he couldn't get enough of. The answer was a hard no. There had never been anyone like her in his life, and he was sure if she were to walk away from him, there never would be again. She was, simply, the woman of his dreams.

He slipped from the bed they eventually made it to and set about making coffee. But his eyes kept turning back to Delilah.

He didn't believe in fate. He didn't believe in the

fantasies he wove in his books. He never thought of himself as fanciful. He was the pragmatic one; the logical one. The one who, given enough time, could find an explanation for everything. He didn't believe Delilah was the woman in Gideon's painting; didn't believe that Delilah was the woman destined to be his the way Trenton had believed that Ginny was his.

But he had no explanation for what Delilah made him feel. He understood love in its basic forms. He knew philia love well, the love he had for his brothers. In some ways, he understood agape love, or a general love of others and their welfare and well-being. He did care about his fellow human beings. Part of that was why he was a teacher. He understood storge love, or unconditional love of family. He loved his mother, despite everything and her choosing her commitment to his father over a relationship with him. But over the years, he had never experienced eros love firsthand; he had never felt this level of romantic love until he'd met Delilah.

Last night had been exhilarating and everything he had dreamed it could be. But it also humbled and frightened him. She had entrusted herself to him. Had given selflessly of herself. But he was afraid. Afraid to believe that she could come to love him the way he loved her. Afraid to believe that when they were back home, and life went back to the way it was, she wouldn't once again withdraw from him.

He watched as Delilah stirred under the covers. She was lying on her stomach, her face pinched, and her breathing was ragged. Realizing she was in the throes of a nightmare, he crossed over to her. Gently, he rubbed her bare back. When she stirred under his touch, he rolled her onto her back, mindful of her leg.

"Isaac?" Lilah's eyes opened, the remnants of the dream fading.

Isaac kissed her lightly but tugged the covers up over her bare breasts to remove the temptation. "You were dreaming."

Lilah rubbed her eyes. "The dreams are all mixed up."

Isaac climbed back into the bed and brought her against his body. "How?"

Lilah laid her head on Isaac's chest, her fingertips digging into his chest. "I was dreaming about when you were in the hospital. There was a woman there I didn't know. She was speaking some language I didn't understand, but I knew she was threatening you. I tried to stop her, but she pulled out a gun and shot you. But I was sitting in the corner, and I couldn't move. I couldn't stop her."

Isaac held her trembling body to his, rubbing his hands up and down her back. "It was just a dream. We're safe here."

Lilah sniffled. "I remember how scared I was when you were in the hospital. All I could think was that you never should have been outside. Trenton had walked me out to my car and was out in the open. You came outside and saved him. But you could have been killed. While you were in the burn ward, I swore I'd find the man who did that to you. When we were allowed to see you, it hurt so much to see you like that."

Isaac gazed down at her. "You were there? I thought I

had dreamed it."

Lilah hugged him closer. "I was there. But I couldn't sit and do nothing. I felt like it was my fault. I had to find him. Freya found him, and his mother found me instead."

Isaac didn't know how to soothe her. "Why would you think it was your fault?"

Lilah lifted her head and gazed into his eyes. She touched the scars next to his damaged eye. "I had drawn these. These look exactly as I drew them for the game."

Isaac wasn't sure what to say to that. But his mouth opened before he could think of something comforting to say. "That's illogical, and you know it."

Lilah shook her head. "Any more illogical than Gideon's paintings?"

Isaac brushed the tears from her cheeks. "Gideon sees Penny in the painting because he unconsciously drew her for his character. Trenton needed the painting as an excuse to act on his unwanted feelings for Ginny. I don't need a painting. I wanted you before I ever saw those pictures."

Lilah brushed a kiss on his mouth. "How many redheads do you know, Isaac? After last night, I'd like to think I'm the woman in the painting."

Isaac set her away from him but kept his eyes steady on hers as he sat up. "I love you, Delilah. But I don't believe in magic or fantasy. I don't believe in dreams being a form of precognition. I believe I have wanted you since I met you. And I believe I see you in that painting for the same reason Gideon saw Penny in his. Because I want it to be real."

Lilah sat up and turned her back to him, grabbing her nightgown.

"Delilah?"

Lilah grabbed her crutches and stood. "At least you believe in love."

Isaac came around to her side of the bed, fearful of what he'd see in her eyes. She was smiling at him through the last of her tears. The fist in his gut loosened. "I do."

She brushed a kiss to his chin. "Good. I think we should get out today, like you suggested. I'm feeling very emotional right now, and trust me, you don't want me blubbering all over you."

Isaac stepped back as she made her way to the bathroom. It hadn't gotten past him that she had not said she loved him. He knew it was too soon. He should have kept it to himself.

He followed her and spoke through the closed bathroom door. "I'm sorry if I embarrassed you by telling you that I love you."

With an exasperated oath, Lilah opened the bathroom door. "You did not embarrass me. I might have embarrassed myself telling you that I felt like I did that to your face, but you telling me you love me did not embarrass me. Confused me, perhaps. Thrilled me, for sure. But we've got plenty of time to figure this relationship out, and I don't think we should rush things any more than we already have. So let me go to the bathroom; we'll eat breakfast, go for a drive, buy things we don't need, and come back and make love. Okay?"

All Isaac could muster was a nod before she closed the door in his face.

Chapter Nine

The small town Isaac had driven them to catered to the ski crowd. With fresh snow, the town was bustling. Right now it was cold, and the skies promised more snow would start to fall any time, but there were no flakes as of yet. Lilah watched from where she sat as Isaac perused the bookshelves of the small gift shop. They'd wandered the quaint shops and had lunch at a quiet restaurant where they'd chatted about inconsequential things. Her leg was hurting, and her armpits hurt from the crutches, but she wasn't ready yet to go back to the cabin.

What they didn't do was pick up talking where they had left off that morning. She had been feeling off balance from the dream. She'd told him things she never planned to tell him. It had been on the tip of her tongue to tell him that she loved him. She did. As crazy as it was, as fast as it had happened, she was in love with Isaac. But some part of her felt he wasn't ready yet for her to share her feelings with him. She had this feeling he wouldn't believe her. No doubt he'd taken his time to come to the conclusion he was in love with her. He'd probably pondered it, rolled it over in his mind, and considered the various outcomes.

She remembered her dad telling her that he'd fallen in love with her mother the moment they met. He had also told her that he had to have patience with her mother to catch up with him. And of course, she had.

She watched as Isaac took the satellite phone out of his

pocket. Their cell phones were off, so she had given her mother his number. She grabbed her crutches and started to rise when he saw her. She could tell he saw the concern on her face when he smiled at her and shook his head. Relieved it was not her mom, she took her time getting to her feet. She maneuvered to where he was.

He finished texting and slipped the phone back in his pocket. He laid a hand on her back as she came beside him. "Ready to go?"

She nodded. "Find anything good?"

Isaac set the book back on the shelf. "I was just browsing. They have a decent selection of audiobooks if you're interested."

She stood on her tiptoes and kissed his cheek. At his questioning look, she responded. "You looked horrified when I told you I listen to books. It's sweet you'd look for me."

Isaac held the door to the shop for her. "I thought about it. Anything that fills your mind with knowledge can't be bad."

Lilah was careful as she made her way back to the car. "What if it's trash?"

Isaac kept a steadying hand on her back. "I have read some terrible books. But the way I see it, if the author went to all the trouble of writing it, there's got to be something redeeming in it."

Isaac helped her settle into the passenger seat. She waited until he started the engine before speaking. "Who was on the phone? Freya or Gideon find anything?"

Isaac shook his head. "Nothing from them. But I

messaged someone. Someone I can trust. He offered to help and agreed to do some digging of his own. Freya and Gideon don't have the resources he does."

"What's his name?"

Isaac slipped on his sunglasses. "We just called him Jones."

Lilah wrinkled her nose. "Sounds like something out of a spy movie."

Isaac shrugged. "It's about what he amounts to. He also has a vested interest in finding Avery. It's the first possible sighting of her in years."

"Why does he have a vested interest?"

Isaac kept his eyes on the road. "The man Avery killed was his younger brother. I was working with Jones, but I didn't know he and Thomas were related. Because I witnessed Thomas's murder, Jones took a personal interest in me. Thankfully he determined I wasn't involved with the murder of his brother, or I wouldn't be sitting here right now."

Lilah shivered. "It all sounds so unbelievable. I still can't believe you never told your friends."

"As you already know, they have their own demons. If they had known I was in the crosshairs of a killer, they would have descended on the mission."

Lilah set her hand on his knee. "And you wanted to protect them."

Isaac nodded. "Let's grab groceries before we head back."

After groceries were done, Lilah was ready to put her leg up. She massaged the ache in her thigh as Isaac drove.

He noticed and frowned. "We overdid it today."

Lilah shook her head. "We needed to get out. And you're going to cook a fantastic dinner while I sit and watch."

His eyebrow cocked at that. "You're getting awfully good at supervising. Do you cook?"

"For me and my mom. I found all sorts of recipes online with antioxidants and anti-inflammatory properties. Lots of fruit and raw foods. But it's nothing like what you whip up."

"Then it's a good thing I like to cook. I hear the way to a woman's heart is through her stomach."

Lilah laughed. "No arguments from me."

He pulled into the long drive that led to the cabin. He suddenly stopped. The road was a straight shot, and there was a large black truck parked near the cabin. He leaned over and pulled the Glock out of the glove compartment.

Lilah undid her seat belt, but his hands stopped her from opening her door. "Stay here."

Lilah was about to argue but saw the hard look in his eyes. She had a feeling she was either going to voluntarily stay here, or he'd make her. She shivered. "What if there is more than one person in there?"

He ignored her. "Keep the doors locked and the lights off. Slide into the driver's seat. If you hear a gunshot or anything that frightens you, I want you to drive straight to the police station. You hear me?"

Lilah grabbed his arm. "I'm not leaving you."

He grabbed her and roughly kissed her. "Do as I say."

He didn't wait for her to respond, but turned off the

dome light, opened the car door, and made his way toward the cabin. It took some ingenuity, but she managed to get into the driver's seat. She tried to quiet her heartbeat and calm her breathing.

She had no choice but to wait.

* * *

Isaac pulled off the tinted glasses and put the clear glass lenses on that he had in his pocket. He kept the Glock pointed at the ground as he circled the property. He stayed alert to any noise in the woods, in case he was being watched, but he didn't hear anything. It was dark; the snowstorm that was predicted was maybe an hour away, and the woods were silent.

He could see through the partially closed curtains that a fire was going. He had put it out when they left that morning. Isaac eased closer, keeping to the shadows. He sidled up to the window. Inside there was a large, black-haired man reading one of the books that Isaac had left in the living room. He could see there was a gun on the table, along with a cell phone. The gun was within reach of the large man, but the man's posture on the couch suggested he was relaxed.

Isaac figured he had two choices. He could simply walk through the front door, gun drawn. Or he could go around back and see if he could get the window in the bathroom open. But the risk of being heard was too great. He eased around the corner of the house. With a powerful kick, the door flew open.

Isaac stood in the doorway, gun locked dead center on the man's heart. The man didn't even jump at the sudden intrusion. He simply set the book in his lap and looked at him. Isaac's eyes narrowed. "You've got five seconds to tell me who you are."

The man closed the book. "Names Jones. Go ahead and check my phone."

Isaac kept the gun trained on the man. He picked up the phone. "Code."

"1990. The year my brother was born."

Isaac punched the code. He then set the phone down and dropped the muzzle of his gun to the floor. "I didn't expect you to show up on my doorstep. How did you even know where my doorstep is?"

The man gave him a shuttered look. "You forget who you're talking to."

Isaac nodded. "I've got to go get Delilah."

Isaac tucked the pistol into the back of his jeans and headed back outside. Delilah was sitting in the driver's seat; her fingers had a death grip on the steering wheel. When she saw him, she opened the door. "Thank God. Who is here?"

Isaac came over and grabbed her by the waist, lifting her from the SUV. He leaned in the back and snagged her crutches. "An old friend."

Lilah used his shoulder for balance as she got the crutches under her arms. "Monroe or Jones?"

"Jones."

He held the door for Delilah as she made her way up the two steps and into the cabin. He watched as she turned violet eyes on their intruder. She didn't say anything as she made her way to the bed and took a seat. Isaac came over and lifted her leg onto a pillow so she could rest it.

Jones watched the couple. "Sorry for the intrusion. It was cold, so I came in and started a fire. I heard you pull into the drive."

Isaac set his gun down on the kitchen counter. "When you said you were looking into it, I didn't expect you to turn up. Certainly not here."

The man shrugged his massive shoulders. "I've been living in D.C. It made sense to stay near our mutual friend. So I was only an eight-hour drive away when you texted last night."

Lilah spoke from the bed. "How did you know we were here?"

The man shrugged again. "Process of elimination. Hotel records and hospital records indicated you were likely in this area. A dig into Isaac's life showed he had a friend out this way. Easy enough from there."

Lilah looked at Isaac. "You said you didn't use your real name during the assignment."

Isaac nodded. "We shared what we knew after the mission ended, including our names. First time we've met, though."

Lilah looked at the man. He was several inches taller than Isaac. His hair was jet black, with a tint of blue. The sapphire-blue eyes sparkled in the light of the fire. "What do we call you? Jones?"

The man twisted his lips into a small smile. "Caleb, ma'am. But I go by Jones."

Isaac threw a couple more logs on the fire. "This is Delilah."

Jones glanced at her, then back at Isaac. "Yours?"

Isaac's lips curved, and he didn't dare look Delilah's way. "Yes."

The man nodded. "Did you see Avery?"

Isaac took a seat between Jones and Lilah. "No. But she's the only one who would want me dead. I'm a teacher. I don't make enemies."

"I saw the attack on Dr. Brandt on the news. I didn't put two and two together right away. Of course, it has been fifteen years, and I only ever saw your photograph. Our mutual friend said that after you were done recuperating, you never came back for a second assignment."

Isaac could only nod. "I'd had enough after that. Rumors are you stayed. Are you still in?"

"Recently retired."

"I can't one hundred percent say it was Avery. There were two of them. They ran my SUV off the road. There was no way for them to confirm our deaths without climbing down a treacherous ravine. They waited a while before finally leaving."

Jones gestured to Lilah. "That the only injury?"

Lilah rubbed the spot on the back of her head but didn't say anything.

Jones saw the gesture, then turned his full attention on Isaac. "How bad is your vision? You managed to sneak up on the cabin without making a sound."

"I can see out of one eye with glasses. The other is just a dark blur."

"We're going to have to use you as bait to draw her out. I'm a ghost."

Lilah perked up on the bed. "He is not."

Jones turned cold eyes her way. "There really isn't a choice. He won't be safe until she's caught or dead. I'll let you guess which I'd prefer. And if you two are close, and she knows it, you're a target by association. She won't hesitate to take you out to get to Isaac."

Isaac growled. "Enough."

Jones stood. "Reality check, Isaac. You know I'm right. You can stay holed up here until she finds you, or you can do something about it."

Isaac gave no sign of what he was feeling. "You're sure you're a ghost?"

The man held out both hands. "Practically transparent. She knows Thomas has a brother. But she only knew me as Jones. You're the only person who knows who I really am. And you two need to keep it that way."

Lilah wrapped her arms around her chest. "Not a problem. I'd like it if you disappeared myself."

The man tipped his head at that. "For now. I'll be back. I've got some feelers out. But the next step is to give it two more days, then send you two home. If we're lucky, Avery will be arrogant enough to show up herself."

They watched as the man left, pulling the busted door shut behind him.

* * *

"I don't like him." Lilah shivered from the bed. The

room was cold, but the man had been glacial.

"No. But he's not here to make friends. I don't have siblings, but I know how he feels. If anything happened to Nash, Gideon, or Trenton, I don't know what I'd do. I don't know what I'd do if something happened to you."

Lilah gestured for him to come to the bed. She cupped his cheek when he sat down beside her. "I know what you'd do. You'd put yourself between me and the danger."

Isaac laid a hand over the fingers that were stroking his scars. "A small price for Trenton's life."

"I guess I agree with that. Though, prison is too good for the man who did this." Lilah shivered as Isaac's arms came around her.

Luke Connor was in jail awaiting trial for not only the attack on Isaac, but also the murders of sixteen people. The judge had not granted bail, so the man was locked up and would never see the light of day. His attorney was holding out and trying to use an insanity plea that his mother had brainwashed him into believing he had to kill anyone related to Hezekiah Stafford, the founder of the cult Trenton had been born into. But he had not stopped with the descendants of the cult leader.

His mother, Katherine, was crazy; there was no doubt. But she knew very well what she was having her son do. And she had been determined to kill the last of the Stafford line, Trenton's stepdaughter Gwenny, or so she thought. She was now raving from her jail cell that she'd kill Trenton and Gwenny.   Hezekiah was Trenton's paternal grandfather, and Trenton had used the information that he was the last of the Stafford line to distract Katherine. The ploy worked, and Trenton stopped her from killing Lilah, Gwenny, and Ginny.

Katherine made a plea deal and would serve thirty years in prison for attempted murder and as an accessory to murder. Now she was also swearing up and down that she killed the sixteen people. But DNA said otherwise. As far as Lilah was concerned, she could rot there until she died. The likelihood of her ever seeing the outside of a jail cell was slim.

Isaac kissed the top of her head. "We'll get Avery out of our lives, and then we can focus on us."

Lilah pulled back. "I'd rather focus on us now."

Isaac pulled her closer, bringing her chest against his. "Do you have any idea how precious you are to me?"

Lilah slipped her hands under his flannel shirt and stroked her palms up his chest. She rubbed her thumbs across his hardened nipples. "I like it when you show me. But right now, I'd rather show you."

Admittedly, she wasn't terribly experienced with men. And it was more than a little challenging to be romantic and try to be alluring when one's leg was in a cast. But Isaac didn't seem to mind or care. He let her take her time exploring the textures of his skin, stripping him of one piece of clothing at a time while trying to keep from hitting him with her cast or falling off the bed.

She stood and balanced on one foot, unhooking one side of her overalls. "It's a good thing I like baggy clothes."

Isaac unhooked the other side and watched as they slid off her hips. "I love watching you take them off."

Lilah smiled and grabbed the hem of her sweatshirt. She

tugged it over her head. She had opted to forgo a bra today, and Isaac's hands covered her breasts. "I have a feeling that there isn't much about me you don't love."

Isaac stood and pulled her hips to his. He touched the hair that fell over her shoulders. "I love your hair."

She tipped her head as he brushed the hair back, exposing her neck.

His lips kissed the skin he revealed. "I love your neck."

Lilah swayed against him.

He kissed her temple, then her nose. "I love your eyes. Beautiful lavender eyes that see things differently from most."

She wrapped her arms around his neck. "What else?"

His fingers trailed down her spine. "I love your hips. The dimples at the base of your spine."

She shivered when his hands caressed her backside, drifting between her legs. "And that?"

His fingers dipped inside. "Especially that."

He lifted her and set her on the bed. "I love your breasts. I love your belly. And your cute knees."

That elicited a laugh. "No one has ever told me I have cute knees."

Isaac curled his fingers around the back of her knees and spread her thighs. He grabbed a condom from the dresser and knelt between her knees, trailing his fingers to her ankles.

She stopped laughing as he curled his hands around her feet, then slid his hands slowly back up her legs. "Isaac. I'm supposed to be seducing you."

He settled against her, cupping his hands under her head.

"Trust me, you are."

Lilah brought her knees up around his hips. Her cast bumped the back of his calf. She lifted her hips and buried her lips in his throat. He kept his hands in her hair as he slowly penetrated her body. She gasped and tightened her thighs around him.

But this time, Isaac wasn't going to be rushed. He kept his pace slow and his touch gentle, rocking slowly back and forth inside her. She dug her nails into his back, but he kept to his pace. She tightened herself around him and ground her hips against his. She was vaguely aware of the mewling sounds she was making, but she didn't care. She begged and pleaded, but he continued the slow rocking. He released her hair, grasped her hips, and ground his against hers. She felt herself shatter.

She went limp under him. He ground his hips against hers one last time and followed.

He lay on top of her, both of them dazed by the intensity of what had happened between them. The depth of feeling.

Isaac lifted his head, licked her lips, and opened her mouth to his kiss. When he came up for air, he looked her straight in the eyes. "There is nothing about you I don't love, Delilah. Nothing."

Lilah felt her eyes sting. She wanted to tell him she loved him, but she held back. His eyes were staring into hers, and she lost her words. But he seemed satisfied with what he saw. He kissed her again before easing away from her.

Lilah turned so she could look at him. She touched her fingers to his lips. "I almost missed out on this. On you."

Isaac's eyes darkened. "I would never have given up."

Satisfied with that answer, she closed her eyes and laid her head on his chest. She fell asleep listening to the beat of his heart.

Chapter Ten

"I really don't like you." Lilah's hands gripped her crutches as she glared at the black-haired man.

Jones simply nodded and sipped the coffee Isaac had poured him. "I get that a lot."

Lilah would have paced, but her leg didn't make that easy. She had to settle for pointing her crutch at him. "If you think I'm going to let you put Isaac in danger for your revenge, you're out of your mind."

Isaac came to her and helped her into a chair. "It's the fastest, most expedient way. Avery doesn't care about you. You can go back to your life while Jones and I track her down. This will be over before you know it."

She glared at Isaac. "You expect me to what, go home and pretend some crazy woman isn't trying to kill you?"

Jones took another sip. "Relationships and sex get in the way. Isaac needs to be objective. You go home. He comes with me. We find Avery. I get my revenge. Then you can have him back. And I'll be gone."

Isaac dropped onto his haunches in front of her. "You can stay with Trenton. Or you can stay with Gideon. Or how about Nash? We can put you up at his parents' house, just like Trenton did with Ginny and Gwenny."

Lilah didn't want to be placated. "And what, the little woman goes and hides and lets the men deal with it?"

Isaac took her hands. "Not any man. Your man. I need to know you're safe. And I haven't come up with a better plan. Jones is right. We can't stay here forever."

But that was exactly what Lilah wanted to do. She knew Isaac was right. And whatever Jones might or might not be, she had a feeling he was a warrior. Something about him reminded her of Gideon. If she were to draw Jones, she'd draw him with a longsword and wearing armor from head to foot.

She ignored Jones and kept her eyes on Isaac. "Why won't your so-called friend help you? Why isn't Monroe looking for her?"

Jones interrupted. "He doesn't want to find her. So long as she stays underground, he can keep the whole thing covered up. The woman sold her soul to the devil a long time ago. She had access to top military secrets and knew where several top-secret U.S. bases were in the Middle East. Good men died. Civilians were killed. The death of dozens sits on her shoulders. But the mission was covered up and excuses for the deaths were made. Families and friends were lied to. Isaac and I are only one of a small handful of people who really know what happened during that mission and the repercussions of its failure. Whether Isaac wants to admit it or not, he wants revenge as badly as I do. And now that she's surfaced, she's not the only one we should be worried about."

Isaac turned angry eyes to Jones. "Enough."

Jones made a chopping motion with his hand into his palm. "We're on the chopping block, whether you want to admit it or not. If we don't find her and silence her, our dear friend might decide to silence us. He's kept this secret for fifteen years. Don't think he won't do everything in his power to keep it that way."

Isaac turned back to Lilah. "We should pack."

Before Lilah could respond, the satellite phone started ringing. She answered it. "Hi, Nash."

Nash's voice was quiet on the line. "Freya has been tracking someone who is looking for Isaac. She hasn't been able to identify him, but she's worried. She said there are so many firewalls and servers bouncing around the globe that she can't get a pinpoint on the person's location or name, but she said he's close."

Her violet eyes darkened. "Yeah, we know. I'm looking at him now. It was a friend of Isaac's, or so Isaac claims. You can tell Freya she can stop tracking him."

Jones smiled. "Your friend is good. Almost as good as I am."

Lilah turned her back on him. "Why did Freya call you? Where's Gideon?"

Nash's tone was back to normal. "Caught a case. A bad one. He's up to his eyeballs at work. So Freya texted me. One of these days I'd like to meet her."

Lilah snickered at that. "You'd have to get her out of her lab first. She's more of a workaholic than you are. And you're pretty bad."

Nash's tone darkened again. "So what's the plan? I assume whoever this guy is that found Isaac is one of the good guys."

Lilah doubted it but didn't say so. "So Isaac says. Their plan is to stash me with you, Trenton, or Gideon, and go all macho and hunt Avery down."

Nash grunted. "Sounds like a good plan. We can stash

you with Penny. My parents are taking a trip, and with Gideon pulling double shifts, she'll enjoy the company. Hand me to Isaac."

Lilah's eyes were narrowed, her temper lit, as she handed the phone to Isaac. She could barely make out Nash's words. Something to the effect of where he should pick her up.

Isaac tucked the phone into his pocket when he hung up. He started packing their things.

She turned her head to look at Jones. He almost looked apologetic. She grabbed her crutches and headed to the bathroom to bag up her things.

* * *

Isaac watched her retreating back.

"Your lady is pretty mad." Jones stayed where he was.

"Yes. This isn't exactly what she signed up for. Give us a few, and we'll be out."

Jones finished his coffee and left the cabin.

Isaac didn't know what to say or do. It was not often he was without words. He knew Delilah was hurt that he was going to leave her and handle this himself. But he couldn't put her in any more danger. And as long as she was away from him, and he was leaving a trail Avery could follow, Delilah would be safe.

He knocked on the door and eased the door open. "Let me help."

Lilah stood at the sink; her head bowed. With a cry, she turned to him and wrapped her arms around his waist.

He closed his eyes as he held her. "I'm sorry, Delilah."

She took a deep breath. "No, I'm sorry. This can't be easy for you. I know you wanted this to stay in your past, and because of things you can't control, the past is now in your present. But I'm scared, Isaac. I don't want to lose you now that I've found you."

Isaac tipped her chin up and kissed her. "This is the best way I know how to keep you safe. All I can say is that in a situation like this, Caleb Jones is the man you want watching your back. And I promise once this is over, things will be back to normal. I'll be the boring professor who lectures, and we'll finish our first graphic novel, which will be a sweeping success. But think about us while we're apart, Delilah. I want the whole package. I hope you do, too. But I will understand if you don't. Things have happened fast over the past few days."

She cupped his hands in hers. "I'll be waiting for you when you get back. The sooner you find her, the sooner we can get back to us."

* * *

Two days. Lilah sat in the bedroom at Penny's house, staring out the window. Her leg had been aching, and she'd used it as an excuse to lie down. It was Saturday, so Penny was at home. Gideon's case wrapped up sooner than he had anticipated, so he too was taking a much-needed day off.

Two days. It was all Lilah could think. She hadn't heard from Isaac since he'd left her at a predetermined spot for Nash to pick her up. Lilah had sat alone in a diner, knowing

Isaac and Jones were nearby, making sure she was safe until Nash arrived. They didn't tell her where they were headed, and a part of her didn't want to know.

Nash had held his arms out to her, and she turned to him for comfort. She choked back her tears. She'd let Nash talk nonsense to her as she settled into the passenger seat and throughout the long drive home.

Two days. It felt like a lifetime.

There was a soft knock at the door. "Come in."

Trenton came in. "Penny said you're feeling pretty down. Thought I'd stop by and cheer you up."

She turned watery eyes his way. "If anyone could, it would be you. But none of us has heard from him. I'm not sure if that's a good thing or not."

"Don't borrow trouble, Lilah. Isn't that what you would tell me?"

She rolled her eyes. "Yeah, that sounds like something dumb I'd say."

Trenton took her hand. "Not dumb. The truth. Isaac is a genius. He'll figure out a way to settle this once and for all. For now, I'd like details."

Lilah opened her mouth but didn't get a chance to speak.

Nash poked his head in. "Me, too. Isaac wouldn't kiss and tell, but maybe you will."

She sniffled. "You two are the best girlfriends a gal could have."

Nash sat on the edge of the bed. "So you've told me. Trenton now I'm not so sure."

Trenton pretended to be offended. "Hey, I'm a great girlfriend. Just ask Penny."

Lilah closed her eyes. "I'm in love with Isaac."

Nash patted her knee. "We know. And we're happy for both of you. You just have to get past this hurdle."

Lilah sat up. "I'd rather talk about Cantwell."

Nash accepted the distraction. "The music is coming along. The composer you recommended is phenomenal."

Trenton seconded that. "Between the team Nash has working on the coding and final development, and the art and music almost done, it's just amazing. I still can't believe we're as far as we are. I've already done a run-through of the game. Plays beautifully."

Nash interrupted. "That's because you're unemployed and can sit around playing video games all day. We still have a few bugs to work out, but the game testers are already at it."

Trenton's brow rose at the first part of Nash's statement but didn't comment. He instead spoke to Lilah. "We hear congratulations are in order. Isaac said Stefan loved your art and signed you immediately."

Lilah shook her head to clear it. "It seems so long ago. I haven't even told my mom yet. I wanted to tell her in person. She's staying with Rob."

Trenton patted her hand. "So I heard. Want to go see her? I can drive you over there."

Lilah knew she'd better get out of this bed before she made a permanent indent in it. A distraction wouldn't hurt. And her mother's shoulder was always available to cry on.

* * *

Two weeks.   Lilah sat at Cantwell's headquarters, otherwise known as Nash's house, and worked at her desk. She'd gone from worried to panicked to whatever she was now. Numb seemed like the right word. Gideon said Isaac had left a message that he was fine. That they were making progress. But the knot in her stomach said otherwise. She wanted to hear his voice.

So instead of worrying and panicking, she worked. Isaac had finished his final draft of the graphic novel, and she had put the rest of her art with it. She spent hours working and reworking the images until they were perfect. She didn't want to send it to Stefan until Isaac was back. So she took Isaac's outline for his second novel and was a quarter of the way through the artwork for that. Sleep eluded her, and she had taken to filling in the story gaps as she went. Likely it would all end up in the trash; she knew she didn't have anywhere near Isaac's talent when it came to writing, but it helped her feel close to him, taking his words and ideas and piecing them together.

When her eyes were crossing and the room spun a little, she leaned back in her chair. She heard Nash come up behind her. He set his hands on her shoulders. "You need to stop, Delilah."

She turned tired eyes to his. "Where is he?"

Gideon came in. "I'm over this. I've talked with my superior. We're going to find him."

Gideon turned on his heel and went down the stairs. Trenton poked his head out of the conference room. "About damn time."

Lilah watched with wide eyes as Nash and Trenton

followed Gideon. She scrambled to her feet, grabbed her crutches, and clumsily followed.

Gideon pulled out his phone. He punched in a number. A woman's soft, smoky voice came over the line. "Hi, Gideon. What do you need?"

Gideon put her on speaker. "Hi, Freya. I want Isaac's location."

The taps of her keyboard came over the line. "He's in D.C. According to the trace on his satellite phone, he's in a shady part of town."

Gideon wrote down the address. "Thanks."

Trenton shook his head. "That's not too far from where our old offices were. What would he be doing there?"

Lilah knew. "Caleb Jones."

Gideon turned. "Who?"

Lilah dropped onto the sofa. "Caleb Jones. That's who he said he was. Isaac said he's a friend from his days at the Pentagon. The man that Avery killed to get at Isaac was Jones's younger brother. He's looking for revenge. Avery, too, when you come right down to it. Isaac was the one who found the proof that she was selling secrets."

Nash paced. "I don't like this one bit."

Gideon seconded that. "Same. Let's go."

Lilah watched as the three men grabbed their jackets. She hopped on one leg and threw herself in front of the door. "This is exactly why he didn't tell you fifteen years ago. He knew you three would come running. He didn't want any of you to get hurt."

Gideon took her by the forearms. "And he ended up being shot. That's not how things are going to end this time."

Lilah paled. "Shot?"

Nash swore. "I guess he left out that part."

Lilah pulled away from Gideon and grabbed Nash's arm. "Shot where?"

Gideon answered. "Shoulder blade."

Lilah thought back to the times she'd seen Isaac without a shirt. It was a lot of times, but other than the time at the pool, when he had a towel over his shoulder, she didn't recall seeing his back. Even at the cabin, he wore a towel over his shoulders. And when they were making love, she wasn't looking at his back. She paled more than she already was.

Gideon steadied her and helped her to the sofa. "We'll find him."

Lilah nodded. "You might want to have Freya let him know you're coming. Caleb Jones strikes me as a shoot-first, ask-questions-later kind of guy."

Gideon nodded and texted as they left.

Nash followed.

Trenton came and kissed Lilah on the forehead. "We'll bring him home. I promise."

* * *

Isaac sat gazing out the window of Jones's house. The interior was sparsely furnished, but it was clean, and despite being often vacant, there were no signs of rodents or bugs. Jones told him the house was under an alias and couldn't be traced back to him. But after two weeks of laying breadcrumbs and basically making himself a target, there had been no sign of Avery. Jones didn't seem to mind the wait. Probably because he didn't have a woman like Delilah waiting for him. In the two weeks they'd been looking for Avery, Jones had admitted to having no family or close ties in D.C. Up until last year, he'd still worked at the Pentagon, though under a different name. When Jones said he was a ghost, he meant it. If he could get in and out of the Pentagon under an assumed identity, there was no telling what secrets he could have learned.

Isaac heard his phone beep. The encrypted number had sent one word. Quartet. Isaac swore.

Jones turned from where he was keeping a similar vigil. "What is it?"

"We're about to have company. And I don't mean Avery."

Jones slapped his hand against the wall. "Your friends, I take it."

Isaac was frankly surprised it took them this long. He'd only given Gideon a week before he came barging in. "It's not like we're having any luck. And we're both tired. We could use more eyes."

Jones turned his back on Isaac. "Gideon, maybe. But you said Trenton was in finance and Nash, well, he's a pretty boy if I ever saw one. I don't need the golden boy and a sissy's help."

Isaac wasn't offended. "They might just surprise you."

Not an hour later, there was a tap at the back door. Both Isaac and Jones had been listening for them. Isaac opened the door and ushered them in.

Gideon took in Caleb Jones. "Delilah was right."

Jones's brow rose, but he didn't reply.

Isaac locked the door behind them. "I take it Freya told you where we were."

Gideon dropped the duffle bag he carried at Isaac's feet. "I told her to keep the trace on you. She's been doing whatever computer stuff she does to scramble the tracker so she couldn't be back traced. No way was I going to let you disappear."

Nash squatted and unzipped the bag. He took out a pistol and tucked it into his waistband. "I take it you two haven't had any luck."

Jones stayed in the kitchen and watched the group.

Trenton glanced his way, then dismissed him. He took the gun Nash handed him. "Freya has also been digging through records. She found a couple of possibilities for you. She's still running background checks."

That caught Jones's interest. "Suspects?"

Gideon nodded. "Freya used to work in the private sector. But a lot of the contracts were government. She has contacts I don't. If Avery is the one who tried to kill Isaac, and we all agree she was, Freya knew she had to be staying nearby. So she dug up Avery's file and worked her way through hotel reservations in the area. This time of year, she would blend in at the resorts, so that's likely where she was. We also know she had someone with her. Freya has been digging into some files of known associates. Files that I'm sure your superiors would rather we not know about."

Jones came further into the room. "And?"

Gideon continued. "She also has been going through

hotel footage to see if her facial recognition software made any matches with the picture she found on file of Avery and the associates Freya has found so far. No hits yet. Unfortunately, some of the hotels have closed-circuit systems, so we would need a search warrant to get to the footage. But we may get lucky."

Jones shook his head. "Your friend is good. I wasn't able to get a hold of Avery's file, though I have accumulated my own data over the years. Give me her info, and I'll send her what I have."

Gideon refused. "Send it to me. And I'll send it to her."

Jones didn't argue. Twenty minutes later, Freya texted Gideon that she had the files.

Nash paced. "We owe her for this. Does she need a car or something?"

Trenton snorted. "You sound like a game show host sometimes."

Nash shrugged. He picked up his phone and took it to the window. "She'll have dinner delivered in an hour."

Gideon approved. "She forgets to eat. Good call."

Trenton blocked Nash to stop his pacing. "So, the cavalry has arrived. What's next?"

Nash turned to Isaac. "Cantwell. Let me call Ginny and see who might want to do a live interview. Gather a nice group for a press conference. Advertise it. Televise it. If you want to be bait, then let's up the game."

Trenton seconded that with one stipulation. "Ginny gets nowhere near that press conference; got it?"

Isaac seconded that. "No one else. Not Penny, not Ginny, and not Delilah."

Trenton took Isaac's arm and turned him to face him. "You haven't asked about her."

Isaac closed his eyes. "I'm afraid to know."

Gideon shrugged behind Trenton's back. "She's a trooper. And she'll be waiting when you get back. But she's wearing herself ragged, working and trying to pretend she's not scared to death. So let's end this."

Chapter Eleven

Ginny had the press conference set up in record time. She protested, of course, that she should be there. After a long and heated argument, Ginny had relented. She did post notice of the live conference and made sure the local press got a hold of the story and posted it on their sites. Gideon was setting up the location, Nash was shopping for clothes, and Trenton was holding down the fort with Isaac and Jones.

Isaac couldn't help but be nervous about his friends being involved. Fifteen years ago he'd kept this secret for all the same reasons he wished he could this time. But he wasn't taking chances with Delilah, and his friends would have his back and take care of her no matter what happened.

Jones joined Isaac and Trenton. "I have to say, I'm impressed. You hit every one of your targets."

Trenton was all teeth and no charm. "Target practice was your idea. You're not a trusting sort, are you? But we're all licensed to carry and can hit what we aim at."

Jones shrugged. "Shooting a crazy woman isn't quite the same as shooting at someone who's shooting at you. But for pretty boys, you and Nash were darn good."

Isaac leaned back and smiled. Jones had insisted they go to the shooting range and practice a few rounds before the press conference. "Gideon was always a natural. He made sure since we were kids that we could defend ourselves. We can handle ourselves and whatever Avery might throw at us."

Gideon came through the back door with dinner. "Everything is set."

Nash followed behind with garment bags. "Everything four grown men need to impress."

Gideon groaned. "He outdid himself."

Nash handed each man a bag. He turned to Jones with a bag. "People on my security team don't wear jeans."

Jones took the bag. He was scowling when he opened it, but he kept his opinion to himself.

Isaac unzipped his bag. The dark navy suit was not his usual style. But he supposed that was why Nash chose it.

Dinner was eaten in silence, and everyone turned in early. Isaac knew everyone's thoughts were heavy. Nash would be mentally centering himself. Martial arts had proved to be a saving grace when it came to calming his mind. Trenton would be counting and tallying figures. Numbers were his specialty. Gideon would be thinking about Penny and focusing on positive thoughts. Isaac would normally be reading, but tonight all he could think of was Delilah.

He'd been telling the truth when he said he was afraid to ask how she was doing. His track record with women wasn't impressive. She was just starting to get used to him and their relationship. They were finding common ground, and he hoped to be building a lasting relationship. He loved her for more reasons than he could articulate. He wanted to marry her. He wanted to have children with her. And he was afraid that while they were apart, she would be rethinking her decision.

Forced proximity had pushed their relationship to the next level. And now they were apart; she was left behind while he dealt with his past. Would she be waiting for him when this was over? He was never a believer that absence made the heart grow fonder. These past two weeks seemed to drag on. He could only be glad that his friends had arrived and were forcing his hand.

Isaac lay in the dark, his thoughts centered on Delilah. He imagined her lying in bed, her face soft with sleep. He hoped that when she dreamed tonight, she would dream of him.

* * *

The morning of the press conference dawned. Nash made sure everyone looked their part, including Jones. In the crowd would be several representatives from various gaming companies eyeing the competition, local enthusiasts who wanted a glimpse of what was gearing up to be the game of the year, magazine writers, and reporters. Chatter among the crowd was filled with enthusiasm and anticipation.

Gideon's boss had several undercover officers milling in the crowd. Gideon had told his captain about Avery and that there was a good chance she was in D.C. Isaac had provided details on what had happened and why Avery was hunting him. Captain Barnes had listened intently, then gave his consent to an operation. As far as he was concerned, she was a threat to national security, and he was going to find her and stop her.

Nash had also hired a security team to hold the crowd back and away from the men. Isaac had been worried about civilians getting hurt. Nash had made sure there was plenty of room between them and the crowd. There would be eyes on every section of the building during the event.

Isaac scanned the crowd. Gideon was watching the crowd. He had insisted everyone wear a mylar vest. Nash had grimaced when he'd been shopping to account for its bulk under the designer suits, but he hadn't argued. Jones stood off to the side of the room verifying IDs of those on the guest list, while each person had their picture discreetly taken and the images fed back to Freya and her team for facial recognition. Live video feed was being monitored by security, as well.

Within the hour, they had taken their places on the stage that had been set up. All four men sat on one side, facing the interviewer. Nash was a natural spokesperson, and he fielded most of the questions. The cameras loved his charcoal-black hair, gray eyes, tan skin, and handsome, angular face. His voice was confident as he spoke about the game while live footage of completed sections of the game were streamed. The enthusiasm in the crowd was palpable.

Gideon had also insisted that each man wear an earpiece. Freya was on a separate line feeding data to them. Another hour went by with nothing noteworthy.

Nash was fully involved in the conversation when Freya's voice came over the line.

"I've got a match. Purple suit jacket, black skirt, silver hair, and silver high heels. Dark red lipstick. Ninety-six percent match to Avery Whitlock. She came in alone. No one else has rung any warning bells."

Jones's voice came over the line. "She's arrogant enough to come alone. I don't have eyes on her."

Freya's voice came over the line as she patched in the live security footage. "Camera four. North side."

Isaac excused himself and left the stage. Gideon followed behind him. Nash and Trenton kept watch from the stage as Nash continued talking with the interviewer. The interviewer watched the two men exit but kept the lively conversation going.

Gideon's exit was the cue to block all entrances. Gideon trailed behind Isaac as he made his way away from the crowd to the monitors nearby so he could see the footage. Isaac took a look at the feed. "That's her."

Jones's voice came over the line. "I still don't have a visual."

The security lead's voice came over. "No visual. She's gone off camera."

Isaac watched as Avery walked out of the camera's view. He scanned the crowd where she had been but saw no movement. Avery was of average height, so she wouldn't stand out. Knowing he needed to draw her away from the crowd, knowing Gideon would not be far behind, he headed behind the area where the small stage had been set up.

He knew the moment she came up behind him.

The woman slipped from the shadows; her gun pointed at Isaac's chest. "You've been a hard man to find, Isaac."

Isaac turned to face her; her gun centered on his heart. She had changed in the past fifteen years. Hair that had once been a deep shade of brown was now mostly silver. More wrinkles lined her face, though the underlying beauty of her youth was still there. Her figure was still trim. But it was her eyes that gave her away. Those blue eyes were still cold. The eyes of a killer.

Isaac slowly walked backward, drawing her further away from the crowd. "I've been waiting for you since the story of my injury aired. I'm surprised it took you six months. Fifteen years ago, you would have been on my doorstep within hours."

Avery kept her steps slow and steady as she followed him. "You made sure I would be on everyone's radar when you messaged Monroe from the hospital. I had to bide my time. My inside man confirmed you had been in touch with him, so I knew then you were the man I wanted. I had to wait until I could get to you some place private, away from D.C. And you accommodated me. I can't believe you survived the crash. Barely a scratch, though I heard your girlfriend wasn't so lucky. Though it does give one pause what kind of woman would date the cerebral Dr. Isaac Brandt. Never fancied you as a teacher when you were younger. But you were dull back then, and it seems you haven't changed."

Isaac kept her talking. "You underestimated me and overestimated your charms. You betrayed your country. You betrayed the men and women under your command. And now that you've made the mistake of resurfacing, you'll finally pay for your crimes."

Avery kept her back toward the wall as she circled him. "I knew you were the mole, but I couldn't prove it. Monroe wasn't keeping his plan a secret, just your identity. You refused to be seduced. But the men helping you find the one who was selling secrets were easy to manipulate. Like Tom. I was able to access your records through his passwords. I knew then I needed to finish the deal and disappear."

Isaac's hands fisted. The memory of Thomas's murder still haunted him. The young man, so eager to prove himself, so eager to serve his country, had been blind to what Avery was. "You didn't have to kill him. He wasn't a threat to you."

Avery laughed. "Dead men can't tell secrets. And you're next."

Isaac shifted his body, opening up a straight line of fire. "I already told your secrets. Killing me won't change that."

Avery's finger tightened on the trigger. "And yet it will be so satisfying."

Jones shifted from where he had been hiding. Isaac's movement was the signal. He pointed his gun at Avery. "Drop your weapon, Avery."

Avery kept her gun on Isaac. "Who are you?"

Jones came closer. "Names Jones."

Avery swore, her arm steady. "You're both dead!"

Avery pulled the trigger, her bullet hitting Isaac square in his chest. She then spun to fire at Jones, but he was faster and shot her in the shoulder. She went down.

Isaac hit the floor and struggled to catch his breath from where the bullet hit the vest, leaving a painful impact to his ribs. He watched as Jones came to stand over Avery, gun pointed at her forehead.

Before Jones could take the shot that would end Avery's life, Gideon drew his weapon and held it to the back of Jones's head. "This is not how this goes down."

Jones growled, anger and his need for vengeance bubbling up. "She killed my brother. Now it's my turn."

Isaac came to his knees. "You and I both know what will happen to her. She'll be convicted of treason, terrorism, and the murder of dozens. She'll be locked away in a place no one has ever heard of. Killing her is giving her an easy out. And there is no telling what else she knows. And there are men who will get those secrets out of her. You know it."

Jones glanced at Isaac, then turned to look at Gideon. "You'd do it, too."

Isaac was relieved when Jones uncocked his gun and stepped away from Avery.

Nash and Trenton came around the corner. Nash saw the hole in the suit right over his heart. "She ruined a perfectly good suit. You okay?"

Isaac nodded, but Trenton and Nash helped him to his feet and started edging him away from the scene.

Gideon gestured to the nearby men, who cuffed Avery and worked to stabilize her until the paramedics arrived. She was swearing up a storm and glaring at Isaac as he left. She shouted at his retreating back. "I know more secrets than you can even guess, Isaac. The question is, can you handle them? Because I don't think you can."

Isaac ignored her. Paramedics came, but he refused them. He let Nash and Trenton help him with the vest. "Get this thing off me. And I need to make a phone call."

Jones came to stand nearby. "Already did. A car will be

waiting for us. Just us."

Nash didn't like that at all. "The same people who said Avery wasn't in the country? That there was no way she was going to surface? Or maybe they want to finish what Avery started."

Jones nodded. "Always a possibility. I never thought Avery was working alone. I had contacts everywhere, but I wasn't able to prove anything one way or the other. Isaac was the only one who found any proof. Frankly, if Isaac were dead, it would be easy to once again bury the whole thing. He was the only one who saw the documents and was able to decipher the codes. Who's to say Isaac wasn't the mastermind and that he set her up?"

Trenton came at Jones and shoved him. "Who the hell are you calling a traitor?"

Isaac laughed, halting Trenton from tearing into Jones. "He isn't. He's right. I am the only one who was able to decipher the codes. And there would be some who would rather see me dead than alive. Fifteen years ago I wasn't sure I'd make it to London to recuperate. But I kept the secrets I knew, and I was left alone. Avery's arrest today won't make the news, and it's in the best interest of national security that Avery disappears. Local police who were here tonight might chat about it, but her arrest will stay under the public's radar."

Gideon tossed the vest and helped Isaac back into his shirt. "There were lots of eyes here tonight. Killing you won't keep this a secret. You can count on it. Your old boss won't have a choice but to deal with Avery and the consequences of her actions."

Isaac let Gideon button his shirt. Hist chest really hurt. "I wonder if Avery will talk? Some of her secrets are ones certain people won't want aired."

Jones shrugged. "I got what I wanted. It's finished."

Isaac watched as Jones headed outside. He turned to his friends. "I have to go. Ask Delilah if she'll meet me at my house. I don't know when I'll be back, but I want to see her."

Trenton hugged him. "I'll take care of Lilah. You go take care of business and put it to bed. For my sake, if no one else's. I don't take kindly to people shooting at my friends."

Gideon walked Isaac out. "It will be interesting to see what story makes it to tonight's news. Nash won't be happy if the press spins it in a way that blames Cantwell for a public shooting. But it could also work in our favor. Never can tell."

Isaac stopped a few feet from where Jones was waiting near a black SUV. "Have Freya keep her tracker on me, would you? Just in case."

Gideon nodded. "You disappear, we'll find you. Count on it."

* * *

It was four in the morning, and he was exhausted. The driver who had picked him and Jones up had returned him to get his SUV. But now, standing outside his darkened house, he felt his spirits drop. Delilah's car was not there. He had hoped she would come. That despite having put her through so much these past three weeks, she would be here for him when he needed her. And he did need her. Outside of the quartet, he hadn't needed anyone in years. But she was now indelibly etched into his heart, and her absence made his heart ache.

He reset the alarm but didn't bother to turn on the lights. He went to the kitchen and poured himself a drink. If ever he needed one, he needed one now.

Fifteen years wasn't long enough. Monroe still held the same position he did back then, and Isaac had thought he'd never have to lay eyes on him again. The man was a civilian and didn't carry a military ranking, though Isaac had no doubt the man had served during his years of service. Monroe told him that Avery Whitlock would be transferred to a maximum-security facility after she was interrogated. He offered no apologies or excuses. Truth was, if Avery weren't in a holding cell, he would still be denying her presence in the U.S. He was less than thrilled with him and Jones catching her. All he would say was that she would be dealt with.

His phone beeped and he checked the message. Per Freya, Gideon was aware he was now home. And that she'd keep the trackers on, just in case. He replied affirmatively and tossed the phone on the counter. He swallowed his drink in one gulp and poured another. After a few minutes, the buzz of the alcohol had gone to his head. Not one to drink hard liquor, it hadn't taken much. But maybe he could sleep. He'd not gotten more than brief snatches of sleep each night the past two weeks.

He turned when his phone beeped again. Trenton. He texted back that he was fine and headed to bed. He smiled at Trenton's sarcastic remark back to him and figured he'd better take the phone with him. He sent a message back to Trenton to tell everyone else he was fine and was going on do not disturb until the morning.

Slightly dizzy, but pleasantly so, he made his way up the stairs. He stripped as he made his way to his room. The darkening bruise on his chest made him wince. Being shot in the shoulder had hurt. But damn if this didn't hurt just as bad. It hurt to take a deep breath.

Naked, he tossed the covers back on his bed. A soft yelp greeted him.

Lilah sat up, her hand to her chest. "You scared the daylights out of me. I didn't hear you come in."

Isaac took a step back. "Delilah?"

Her eyes narrowed. "It better be, or you're in trouble. Just how many women did you invite over here?"

Isaac grabbed her arms and tugged her to him. She stumbled a bit in her cast as he pulled her to her feet, but he kept a firm grip on her. She was wearing one of his pajama tops, and from what he could tell, nothing else. "I didn't think you were here. Your car isn't here."

She cupped his face in her hands. "Of course, I came. You asked. Not that you needed to ask. Trenton drove me."

Struggling to find the right words to say to her, he grabbed her hips, pulling her flush against his naked body. "I need you."

Lilah used her weight to pull him down onto the bed with her. "I need you."

Isaac groaned, but not in pleasure. He clutched his chest and ribs before getting back on his feet.

Lilah saw where his hand went. "What happened?"

His eyes narrowed when she snapped the bedside table lamp on. "Bullet."

Lilah paled. "What?"

Isaac cursed his loose tongue. "I'm fine. I was wearing a vest. All part of the plan."

Lilah got to her knees. "Your plan was to get shot?"

Isaac shrugged his tense shoulders in a very Nash-like move. "Sort of. I knew we had to draw her out. And she would smell a trap. So wearing a vest, I wandered off with Jones and Gideon not far behind. She shot me, Jones shot her, just a flesh wound in the shoulder, and Gideon kept Jones from shooting her again. Avery is in custody. She got a quick patch job and then was taken away."

Lilah touched the forming bruise with light fingers. "Nash told me she was caught. But he left out some important details."

Isaac knelt beside her on the bed. He once again pulled her to him, so she was sitting beside him. "Not important. I'm fine. She's caught. And I can go back to my real life. And if you give me a chance, I want you to be part of that real life. I know it wasn't fair making the choices I did to leave you to catch Avery. But I had to if I was ever going to be free of my past."

Lilah gently pulled him closer and helped him lie on his back. She straddled his hips, the cast not making it easy.

Isaac's hands crept under her shirt. "I knew you were naked under my shirt."

Lilah leaned over him. "Were you drinking?"

Isaac's fingers caressed her backside. "I thought you

weren't here."

Lilah gave him a lopsided smile. "That's sweet. Are you drunk?"

Isaac's fingers curved around the inside of her thighs. "Not too drunk to satisfy you."

Lilah's eyes closed as his fingers found her core. "So I see."

Isaac teased her until she was writhing against his hand. "Condom in the drawer."

Lilah leaned over, her body partially taking him inside her. She moaned but leaned over just enough to get the condom, but not so far as to take him fully inside her.

Isaac's body hardened under hers. The urge to ignore the condom and take her made him break out in a sweat. "Now, Delilah."

She eased off and rolled the condom on. Without hesitation, she took him fully inside her. They both moaned in unison.

Isaac knew he wouldn't last long. His chest muscles hurt too much, so he let her fully take the lead. He closed his eyes, savoring every moment. He held back until he felt her convulse around him. Gripping her hips, he pulled her firmly against him, grinding himself against her until he came.

Lilah carefully eased off him, rolled the condom off, and hobbled to the bathroom to dispose of it. "That looks really bad."

Isaac held his hand out to her. "Didn't feel a thing. You're still wearing my shirt."

Lilah slowly unbuttoned the shirt and let it fall to the

floor. "Better?"

Isaac pulled her to him and sighed when she pressed her bare breasts against his chest. "Much."

Lilah laid her palm over his heart. "Want to talk about it?"

"No. But I guess you deserve to hear it. My ex-superior is not too pleased right now. He would have preferred Avery to remain missing. No doubt he'll have to explain her reappearance to his superiors. Avery is going to do what she does best, and that's play games and lie. She was taunting us that her secrets were too valuable. And maybe they are."

Lilah rubbed her palm on his chest in soothing circles. "I've seen movies. Do you think she knows enough to get a deal?"

Isaac yawned. "I hope not. But my mission and the information I found were probably the tip of the iceberg, so to speak. She spent a lot of years in the military. No telling how many people she knows, how many people she betrayed, and how many people besides me and Jones have been looking for her over the years. Either way, she'll be dealt with. If she gets a deal, she'll have no choice but to disappear for real this time. And if she doesn't, she'll rot in prison. All I care about is that she's not my problem anymore."

Lilah kissed his chest. "I hope so."

Isaac pulled her closer and looked at her mouth. "I know so. I forgot to kiss you."

Lilah brushed her mouth over his. "I can fix that."

Isaac cupped a hand behind her neck so that he could

kiss her back. He wanted a taste, a real one. Her mouth opened to his, and he forgot about everything else but the woman in his arms. "I seem to be doing this backward tonight."

Lilah giggled into his mouth. "That just means we get to go forward this time."

Afterward, with Lilah collapsed at his side, Isaac murmured his love for her, and he fell asleep.

Chapter Twelve

Life was back to normal. Or as normal as it got, Isaac supposed. He was back to teaching. He had a new batch of students, had updated his curriculum, and was working on a new novel. Spring break was coming up, and he had hopes he could convince Delilah to go away with him for a few days. They both had been working hard to get the first graphic novel completed, and the beta testing of the game had been expanded. Early reviews were in, and they had an early success on their hands.

Delilah was back at her apartment with her mom, though if he could convince her to come away with him, moving them in with him was the next part of the plan. He'd been true to his word, and he'd helped Delilah and her mom while Delilah's leg had been in a cast. She was now out of it, and her leg was fully healed. Her mom was still dating the doctor, and it made him smile at how uncomfortable Delilah still was when she talked about her mom's relationship. She was hinting that she thought wedding bells might be imminent.

Isaac wanted to ask Delilah to marry him, but he held back. She still hadn't told him she loved him. And while he was pretty sure she did, he couldn't ask her until she did. But at least he had her mother on his side. She approved of their relationship. She had looked him in the eyes and declared he was the one. And he genuinely liked her. Delilah didn't look much like her mother, except for the eyes. The red hair and fair skin were her dad's, but those lovely lavender eyes were from her mother.

Isaac wrote a few more paragraphs before looking at his watch. His next class started soon. Delilah had given the watch to him for his thirty-ninth birthday. She'd blushed a bit, and he had to stop her when she apologized for it not being as nice as the one that had been stolen. The watch could have been a cheap dime store version, and he'd have loved it. But the steel watch was practical, and since Nash had helped her pick it out, it was fancier and more stylish than he'd have bought for himself.

"Class soon?" Gideon knocked on his office door.

"What are you doing here? Is everything okay?" Isaac grabbed his notebooks and textbooks. It was rare for any member of the quartet to show up at the university.

Gideon stepped in and closed the door. "Everyone is fine. But I wanted to talk to you, and I didn't want to bring it up in front of the others."

Isaac set the books down. "I really hope we're not about to talk about who I think we're going to talk about."

"Sorry, man. Freya couldn't leave it alone. She's been digging in her free time."

Isaac closed his eyes. "I've not heard anything from Monroe. Jones, either. My hope is that Avery is locked up tight somewhere."

Gideon rubbed the bridge of his nose. "She's locked up, as far as I've been able to find. Once she was taken out of MPD custody, she became a ghost in the system. But Freya said there's been some odd chatter among the people she's been monitoring. Remember when I said she hoped to find where Avery and her partner were staying in hopes of pinning down who helped her run you off the road?"

Isaac groaned. "How could I forget? She found him?"

Gideon nodded. "But it's a her. A woman named Ramona Levinson. I didn't want to show the picture to Delilah without talking to you first. But she fits the general description of the woman who lifted her key card and broke into your hotel room."

Isaac swore. He took Gideon's phone and looked at the woman. "She'd be the right age. Right hair color. Damn. Where is she?"

Gideon took the phone. "Right now, she's in California. Living the high life in Sacramento. She's shacked up with a guy named Santiago Sanchez. He owns a very popular Mexican restaurant, and the way Freya sees it, she uses him for an address and likely a few other things. Freya said he's harmless: no record, no shady history. Guy's life is an open book."

Isaac looked at the picture. "Avery was always good at seducing young men. This guy doesn't look a day over twenty-five."

"Twenty-four."

Isaac sighed. "I guess I should be glad she's in California and not D.C. Maybe Avery paid her to help. I take it Freya didn't find a personal connection."

Gideon shook his head. "No connection at all. Freya has not been able to find a money trail between Avery and Ramona. But that doesn't mean there isn't one. For now, Freya is tracking her to make sure she doesn't make her way here or anywhere near you or Delilah."

Isaac watched as Gideon turned darkened eyes to stare out the window, as if his mind were far away. That was never a good sign. "What else?"

Gideon rolled his shoulders and brought his attention back to Isaac. "I don't know. Just a feeling."

That was one thing Isaac couldn't explain away, no matter how much logic he applied to it. Isaac knew to take Gideon's feelings seriously. They were usually on the mark. "Avery is in jail. I don't know this Ramona, and I can't imagine she's got so much loyalty for Avery that she'll risk being exposed. She has to know by now that Avery was caught."

Gideon tucked the phone in his pocket. "What should I tell Freya? Show Delilah, or pretend she didn't find it and discreetly keep an eye on her?"

Isaac wanted this over and wasn't willing to stir the pot. But neither was he naïve. "Keep an eye on her. She stays away, we'll keep it to ourselves. Monroe won't thank me for it, and Avery was the one calling the shots."

Gideon gave the office a once over. "I don't know how you don't suffocate in here."

Isaac grabbed his books. Two walls were covered in bookcases loaded with books, and a worn, brown leather couch was shoved against the other wall. His desk sat in the middle. "I like the ambiance."

Gideon shook his head and walked with Isaac to his classroom. "Just be careful. Keep an eye out for anything unusual."

Isaac promised and went inside.

Classes went well, but Isaac was more than ready to call

it a day once his last class ended. He was picking Delilah up for dinner. They'd been playing at dating for the past few months. Some nights he could coax her to come home with him, but she always left afterward to be with her mom. As much as he wanted to spend the whole night with her, he understood. But maybe it wouldn't hurt to start pushing her into a real commitment. Just a little push.

He arrived at her apartment shortly after five. Priscilla answered the door from her wheelchair.

"Isaac, come in. Lilah's almost ready."

Isaac turned to see Delilah coming out of her room. He swore he stopped breathing. She wore a calf-length turquoise blue dress. The textured bodice was form-fitting with a flowing skirt. She had on dress flats, but they were silver instead of her usual black, more functional ones. Black stockings completed the look. Her red hair was up in a twist, with a few tendrils flowing down her cheeks.

Lilah smiled at him. "I'm ready to go."

Isaac had to find his voice. "You look different."

Lilah smirked at her mother. "See what I mean. Have fun. I'll see you Monday."

Priscilla took and patted Isaac's hand. "You two have fun, too."

Isaac took Delilah's elbow and walked her to the elevator. "Did I miss something?"

Lilah wrapped her arms around his neck and kissed him in plain view of anyone who could be watching. She pulled back and smoothed her palms over his chest. "You didn't miss anything. I just wanted to see that look on your face."

Isaac smoothed his palms over her hips. "The one where

my tongue hangs out of my mouth?"

She lightly kissed him. "That one. We should eat. I'm starving."

Isaac halted her when she turned. "You always look beautiful to me. But tonight you look amazing."

She smiled and tipped her head. "I like how you said it in the apartment."

Isaac spoke again in the elevator. "I don't always say the right thing."

Lilah laid her head on his shoulder for a brief moment. "I like how you say things."

An hour later, after they finished their meal, Isaac led her to the restaurant lounge for a drink. "So you said to your mom that you would see her Monday?"

Lilah tucked her skirt under her and settled onto the stool. "My mom told me that I wasn't putting enough effort into our dates. She watches me leave with you, and she pointed out that not once did I put extra effort into my appearance. You always look nice. And I realized she was right. Though not necessarily for the same reasons."

Isaac ordered their drinks and then turned back to her. "Reasons?"

Lilah wet her lips. "She thinks I need to stop dancing around you and let you catch me. I've been thinking about it."

Isaac's mouth went dry. "Catch you?"

Lilah turned on the stool, her eyes unsure. "Rob asked her to marry him. They're eloping this weekend."

Isaac knew laughter was not the proper response. But that's the only one he had. "Delilah, you're sweet and a great daughter. But I'm on team Priscilla. Life's too short. You said she loves him and that he loves her. And they're not kids."

Lilah wiped a tear. "I'm not either. But I think I've been acting like one. I didn't know how to let her go. She and my dad were always there for me. And Mom and I clung together when we lost him. After she got sick, survival was all I could think about. How was I going to keep us in the apartment? How was I going to keep food on the table? I never told you, but Cantwell kept us from being homeless. I was at my wit's end. I made Trenton promise not to tell any of you because I didn't want anyone to know how bad things had gotten. And I realize now that it was silly."

Isaac didn't know what to say to that. "You relied on her. And she relied on you. She will still rely on you, even if she's married to and living with Rob."

Lilah put her hand on his knee. "I know. And it's a good feeling to know she's fallen in love again. And Rob really is a great guy. He's funny, a little quirky, and nothing like my dad, other than he is someone you can rely on. So I'm happy for her. I really am."

Isaac brought his lips to her ear. "So does that mean I get to keep you tonight?"

Lilah wrapped her arm around his waist and turned her mouth to his. "Tonight, tomorrow night, the next night, etc."

Isaac pulled back. "Are you going to move in with me?"

Lilah leaned forward and kissed him ever so lightly. "I want you to catch me. So you tell me?"

Isaac dug out his wallet, pulled a few bills out, and tossed them on the bar. "Let's go."

Lilah barely had time to grab her purse before he led her out of the lounge. She was giggling as they walked briskly to the car. "Slow down. I'm not going anywhere."

Isaac spun and was ready to whisk her up in his arms and carry her to his car when he heard a voice call his name.

Ice filled his veins at the sound of that voice. Pulling Delilah to his side, he turned. "Dad."

"Isaac." The much older man was the same height as Isaac, his hair once the same blond color. He gestured at the petite woman beside him. "Your mother saw you leaving the restaurant and wanted to say hello."

Millicent Brandt glanced at her son and the woman beside him. "Who's your friend?"

Isaac realized he couldn't just walk away. "Mom, this is Delilah Fitzpatrick. She's my girlfriend."

The silver-haired woman held out her perfectly manicured hand to her. She gave Lilah a small smile. "Nice to meet you, Delilah."

Lilah took her hand. "Nice to meet you."

Isaac put his arm around her waist. "This is my mother, Millicent, and my father, Dr. Theodore Brandt."

Isaac wanted to smack his father's hand when he held it out to her.

Dr. Brandt looked her over as he released her hand. "Do you work at the university?"

Lilah glanced up at Isaac. "No. We met through mutual friends outside the university."

"Those three hoodlums he calls friends, no doubt."

Lilah's mouth dropped open. "Hoodlums?"

Isaac shook his head at his father. "Yes, my friends. I'm sure you've got much more important things to do than chat with me."

Millicent laid a hand on his arm. "I hope you're doing better after your accident. I heard about it on the news. It was just awful."

Lilah's mouth tightened. "Most mothers would have come and seen for herself. Fathers, too."

Dr. Brandt's stance changed. "Don't take that tone with me, young lady. I can see why my son would be with the likes of you. No doubt you two are in a hurry for a night of hedonism."

Lilah sputtered and looked at Isaac. Then she turned angry eyes on the man. "As a matter of fact, we are. So if you'll excuse us. Mrs. Brandt, it was nice to meet you."

Isaac let Delilah drag him off. They were out of earshot when she started muttering.

"That's your dad? No wonder you don't talk about him. Hedonism? Seriously?"

"How about lustfulness or debauchery? Maybe depravity?"

Lilah stopped. "It's not funny. He is an ass."

Isaac felt the knot in his stomach loosen and go away. "How about we pick up where we left off? I was about to throw you over my shoulder and carry you off."

Lilah pointed. "Your car is right there."

Isaac opened the door and helped her in. Forgetting the incident with his father, he drove them home.

* * *

Two hours later, Lilah was lying naked and sweaty on Isaac's chest. "Can I just say that hedonism is really fun."

Isaac's laughter rumbled in her ear. "Sure is."

She toyed with his chest hair for a moment. "So the dress was for another reason."

Isaac glanced over. The dress was lying with the rest of her clothes on his floor by the door. He'd stripped her where she stood the moment they got to his bedroom. The stockings ended up being thigh-high, and damn if that wasn't the sexiest thing he'd ever seen. The black panties paired with the thigh-high stockings had been his undoing.

But he sensed a change in Delilah's mood. "What other reason other than you looked sexy in it?"

Lilah sat up. "I wanted to talk about this before we got naked. But you sidetracked me. Thank you, by the way."

He scooted up and propped the pillows behind his back. "You're welcome."

Lilah looked around. "I can't talk to you naked. You're staring at my breasts."

"I can look other places too."

She smirked and went to his dresser. She pulled a t-shirt out and put it on. "I'm serious."

Isaac sat up. "How serious?"

Lilah licked her lips. "So remember when I said I wanted you to catch me?"

Isaac nodded. "Not a thing that a man forgets."

Lilah tugged the hem of the shirt in a nervous gesture. "I've been thinking about us a lot. And I was thinking about things my mom said. And my dad, too. I've felt like I've been in a whirlwind for the past few years. I don't want to say trapped, because I don't think that's the right word. But I've had so many responsibilities, and it seemed like things were never going to change. But they have been for the past year. You've changed things for me. For the good. I knew it was time I stopped dancing around you, but I wasn't sure how. So I bought the dress, got my hair done, and figured we could talk about it."

Isaac leaned forward so he could take her hand and pull her onto the bed. "You're stalling, Delilah. It's not like you."

She felt tears sting her eyes. "I love you, Isaac. I want what you want. I want to grow old with you. Will you marry me?"

Isaac's heart raced in his chest. He could see tears in her eyes, but she was smiling at him. Her lips were curved, and her hands were now strangling his shirt as she waited for him to answer her.

She shrieked when he pulled her down on top of him and rolled her onto her back. His eyes held hers until she was still underneath him. "Yes."

She closed her eyes and wrapped her arms around him. She sniffled into his chest. "I bought a ring."

Isaac braced himself over her. "You did?"

She wriggled out from under him. "I did."

Isaac sat up, unsure of what to say. He had imagined proposing to her a dozen times. Never once had he imagined her proposing to him. She came back with a ring box that had been tucked in her purse. She opened it and showed it to him. He picked up the band. It was a steel band with etchings. He grabbed his glasses from the nightstand.

She knelt beside him. "Cantwell. The etchings are from the designs I made for the game. The woman your character is seeking is kept hidden in a chamber. These designs are etched on the walls of that chamber."

Isaac's thumb brushed against the design. "This is beautiful."

Lilah took his hand that held the ring in hers. "I wanted you to know I was serious. This isn't because of any other reason than I love you. Even if my mom weren't marrying Rob, I'd have found a way to make this work between us. You're not like any man I've known. And my mom was right; I had better snatch you up before some other woman does."

Isaac pulled her to him. "No other woman even comes close. I love you, Delilah. I can't love anyone else."

She laid her head on his shoulder. "Want to run away with me?"

Isaac held her and rubbed her back. "You really think Penny, Ginny, and the Quartet are going to let us?"

She smiled against his neck. "Maybe not. We could not tell them."

He shifted so he could pull the t-shirt off her and settle them under the covers. "How about we compromise, and we get married really soon?"

Lilah took the ring he was still holding. "We have to make it official."

Isaac held his hand out to her and let her slide the ring on his finger. She then curled up against him, laid her hand on his heart, and they fell asleep.

* * *

Lilah swung her foot as she sat on the stool and slowly read Isaac's latest chapters. Isaac was fixing breakfast. "This is really, really good, Isaac. You outdid yourself."

Isaac flipped the pancakes. "You said you had written some stuff, but you've been refusing to show it to me. Since we're engaged, do you think you might finally show me?"

Lilah bit her lip. He'd been asking her about the children's books she had written in college. Now that she knew him better, she realized he wasn't going to forget she'd told him about them. And after Avery was caught, she mentioned she had written some pages based on his outlines and had done some drawings. She had enthusiastically shown him her drawings but had refused to show him the pages she had written.

And she knew they had one more thing they needed to talk about before a wedding took place. "Let's eat, and then we need to talk."

Isaac flipped the pancake on top of the stack. "Last one. Fruit is already cut up, coffee is fresh, and the syrup is hot."

Lilah poured them both a fresh cup of coffee. She mixed his the way he liked it. Mostly milk.

Isaac set the food on the table. "Talk about what? You're not reneging on the engagement, are you? I'm not giving the ring back."

He was smiling at her, obviously not worried.

Lilah fixed a plate and took a bite. "I don't know anyone who makes pancakes from scratch. I'm definitely getting the better deal in this marriage."

Isaac just watched her eat. "You're stalling. Going to show me the pages?"

Lilah sighed and her shoulders dropped. "Yeah. And the books, too. Let's finish breakfast, then we can go to your office."

She lingered over breakfast; it wasn't hard to do when the meal was amazing. She knew when she had the ring made that she needed to tell him why she had been so reluctant to get close to him.

Isaac walked behind her as she climbed the stairs. "We should get another desk in here, so you have your own space. Or we could convert one of the three bedrooms for you."

Lilah looked over her shoulder. "I guess that depends on how many we want to use for kids. You said you wanted kids."

Isaac nodded. "We do have a few things to talk about. Two?"

Lilah stopped on the step above him. She turned and kissed him lightly. "Two sounds good to me. And we probably do want different offices. I work from home a lot, and I tend to be messy when I'm focused. My desk would drive you crazy."

Isaac grabbed her hips. "You already drive me crazy."

Lilah pulled back. "Don't start that, or we'll never talk."

Isaac let her go and followed her the rest of the way.

Lilah grabbed her laptop from the corner of his desk. She turned serious eyes his way. "When I first met Ginny, she asked me why I didn't like you. And it's not that I didn't. You were perfectly nice. But when I heard the word doctor, it put me on edge. And you being the PhD kind didn't make it better. If anything, that made it worse. I was intimidated. Afraid that you might see things that I had managed to hide from all my other employers."

Isaac took a seat. "What would I see?"

Lilah took a deep breath. "That I wasn't good enough."

Isaac protested. "Delilah. If anything, I didn't think I was good for you. Especially after the attack. You didn't need another person to take care of."

She gave him a crooked smile. "It felt nice. It felt nice to be needed by someone other than family. I can't explain it. But I would say we're more than even. You took care of me when my leg was in a cast. And you don't need me to do things for you anymore, not caregiving things, anyway."

Isaac nodded. "I need you for a lot of things, Delilah. And I hope you need me."

Lilah came and wrapped her arms around him. "That's why I love you. You know how to give and take. You're not all macho, and you're not afraid to show how you feel."

Isaac kissed her hair. "Legacy of my father, no doubt. But why did I intimidate you?"

Lilah pulled back. "You're so smart. I mean, I'm not dumb, but I'm not smart like you. I hated school, and you teach. I only got my associate degree, and you've got multiple doctorates under your belt. Who knows how our kids will turn out."

"I'm not worried about that. Like any parent, I just want them to be happy and healthy."

Lilah pulled up the documents she had kept from him.

"Here you go. The top one is one of the kid's books. I have to say my drawing has improved a lot since then. My words, not so much. The one underneath is what I wrote off your outline while you were away."

Isaac took the laptop from her. He was smiling as he looked at the children's story. "A little girl named Violet?"

"Yeah. I was always partial to that name."

His smile started to drop some as he continued reading. He scrolled to the next page and then the next. "You wrote these in college?"

Lilah came and dropped onto the nearby sofa, keeping her eyes on his face. "I'm dyslexic. I could never seem to get my words down on paper. I saw a specialist for about four years through high school. I barely passed. And college was worse. I had tutors to help me, and a couple of friends who would help me polish up my papers before I submitted them."

Isaac set the laptop aside. "The stories are cute. With a little help, you could finish them. We have a great agent. And your words aren't my words, but I like your take on my outline. I've always been impressed with how you can see things that aren't real; put down in pictures the words and give them a new life. Words are important, Delilah. But struggling to get them down on paper is not the same as not having them."

Lilah felt her eyes tear up. "I wasn't sure how you'd feel about me if I told you. But that's my insecurity. Nash said I was perfect for you. That you didn't need someone just like you. I decided he was right. I think I'm the perfect woman for you."

Isaac sat and pulled her into his arms. "You got that right."

<h1 style="text-align:center">Chapter Thirteen</h1>

Nash was working with Lilah the following day. They had gone over the latest batch of beta test results, approved more of the music, and followed up with the third parties they had partnered with to finish the game development.

Nash stretched and turned the topic to personal matters. "So I heard you met Senior the other night."

Lilah scowled. "What an awful man. You should have heard what he said to us. I can see why Isaac avoids him. The only thing those two have in common is their looks. Isaac does resemble his father. His mom seemed okay, but she didn't say much. Honestly, in hindsight, I'm surprised Senior let her acknowledge that she had seen us."

Nash tapped his pen on his pad. "You have a point. I don't think the woman has been allowed to think a thought in her head that wasn't Senior approved since the day they met. She never struck me as a bad person. Just beaten down."

Lilah nodded. "Yeah, that's the feeling I got. I'm sure Isaac won't be inviting them to the wedding."

Nash gave a harsh laugh. "Even if Millicent wanted to come, the second Senior found out, he'd squash the idea. But trust me, Isaac got over the relationship, or lack thereof, with his parents years ago. I take it he loved the ring. I saw he was wearing it."

She smiled at the memory. "He did. I think he was shocked. Isaac does strike me as the traditional type. I am guessing there will be a solitaire diamond in my future. Did he ask you to help pick one out?"

Nash tipped his head. "No. But he should. Isaac might surprise you. You're right about him being traditional. But you know, sometimes I see traditional in you."

Lilah's voice was wistful. "Yeah. I wanted to get married at the same church my parents got married at. But it's not there anymore. I had visions of a white dress and purple roses. But since we can't get married where my parents got married, I've got an idea that's just as good."

Nash waved his hand in a forward motion. "And?"

"The Smithsonian Castle, or maybe one of the museums. It would be perfect to get married surrounded by history. I don't know how quickly we could book a wedding, but it would be a small one, so maybe we could."

Nash's lips slowly curled into a smile. "Let me. The Camhion name can sometimes be useful."

Lilah threw herself at him and hugged him. "That would be amazing. I know you hate to throw your family's weight around, but it's for a good cause."

Trenton came in. "I want in on the action."

Lilah kept her arm around Nash and turned. "We're planning a secret wedding."

Trenton kicked the door closed behind him. "I definitely want in."

An hour later, the three of them had a game plan. Lilah was giddy with excitement. She and Isaac had been talking about when and where they might hold the service, but her idea was perfect.

Trenton was going to handle invitations. Nash was in

charge of clothes and the venue. Lilah knew her next stop was a dress. Nash had some ideas about that, too, and gave her some suggestions. But he happily bowed out when she said she wanted to do that with her mom.

Isaac and Gideon came in and found the three of them huddled together.

Gideon tossed his jacket on the counter and contemplated the group. "Working without us?"

Lilah didn't dare look at Isaac. "No. We're conspiring. Nothing to worry about."

Isaac took Gideon's jacket where he'd tossed it and hung it in the closet. "Any time that word and Trenton are in the same sentence, there is cause for worry."

Trenton laid a hand on his chest. "You wound me."

Isaac looked at Lilah. "Anything I should be concerned about?"

Lilah rose, wrapped her arms around his waist, and lifted herself for a kiss.

Nash groaned. "There is way too much smooching around here. I'm out."

The four of them watched Nash retreat. It was Gideon who spoke. "He looked happy."

Lilah leaned against Isaac. "I gave him a new project to work on. He'll be so focused on it that he won't have time to worry about anything else."

Gideon kept his eyes where Nash exited. "Good. Things have been quiet and back to normal around here. Let's keep it that way."

Trenton raised his right hand. "I swear that if anything abnormal happens around here, it won't come from me."

Isaac snorted. "Yeah, right. You're the one who came up with most of the schemes we've gotten ourselves into over the years."

Trenton tucked his tongue in his cheek. "Not me this time. Let's go eat. I'm starving."

* * *

Everything was perfect. Now all she had to do was tell Isaac. Nash would be here any minute. Isaac's traditional black tuxedo was waiting at Nash's house. Nash had vacillated between tails or no tails, but she had nixed the tails. She'd rather see Isaac in the classic black formal jacket and bow tie. She had also nixed a cummerbund or a vest. Her dress was simple, and she wanted his suit to be, as well.

Nash had come through with a wedding and reception at Kogod Courtyard at the Smithsonian American Art Museum. The space was big enough to set up an area for the wedding and then a reception there as well. Nash had booked a late afternoon so the courtyard would be filled with natural light for the ceremony, and then beautiful lighting in the evening.

She was thrilled Nash had handled the guest list for Isaac. There were friends and colleagues from Georgetown who would be there. Nash's parents were coming, as well as Gideon's mom and sister. On her side, there was her mother and Rob, and a host of gamer and computer friends. Penny and Ginny had accompanied her and her mom, and she found a ready-made silvery-white dress that fit beautifully. The bodice had an overlay of lace, the back was open, and the flowy, slim A-line skirt fell to the floor. The skirt would hide her imminently practical white flat shoes, though they were embellished with some crystals on the top. Both were hidden in the back of the guest room closet.

Trenton had agreed to walk her down the aisle and then stand with Isaac, Gideon, and Nash. Ginny and Penny had agreed to act as her bridesmaids, and since the wedding was small, her mom was her matron of honor. An accommodation had already been made for her mom's wheelchair should she need it. All three women had lovely lavender dresses; her mom's had extra embellishments, and she was thrilled with the purple rose bouquets and boutonnieres.

Isaac had surprised her with a non-traditional amethyst engagement ring. The deep, square-cut amethyst was accompanied by a white gold band with small diamonds embedded. The slim wedding bands they chose fit the styles of both her ring and his. After he had given her the ring, she had convinced him they should get their marriage license, but she had been stalling on committing to a date and place.

Nash's knock was on time. Lilah popped up from her seat in the kitchen where they were eating breakfast. "I'll get it."

Lilah practically ran to the door. "Thank goodness. I'm a nervous wreck. Isaac's in the kitchen."

Isaac came out to the doorway. "He's right here. What is going on? Everyone has been acting secretive, and might I say, evasive."

Lilah, still in her blue bathrobe, looked at Isaac through her lashes. She then came and laid her hands on his chest.

"We're getting married today."

Shock was a mild word for the expression on his face. Then his eyes darkened, and he grasped her to him. Bodies pressed together; his lips descended on hers. His fingers surged into her hair, holding her while the passion of their kiss grew.

A small cough filled the entryway. Lilah pulled away from the kiss that was quickly getting out of control. She turned her head and saw Nash's back. He was studying a picture on the wall.

Lilah gave him one last hard kiss. "Go get dressed. My mom, Penny, and Ginny will be here soon. Nash is taking you to his house to get ready. Gideon and Trenton will meet you there. I'll see you at four."

Nash had Isaac out the door in record time. Lilah leaned against the door and then ran up the stairs. She had a wedding to get ready for.

* * *

Isaac sipped his champagne as he watched Delilah take turns dancing first with Trenton, then Gideon, then Nash. She was now dancing with Rob while he stood to the side with the quartet. He had thoroughly enjoyed their first dance as husband and wife. After two minutes of his hands on her bare back, he'd been ready to leave. But of course, the reception was just starting.

Isaac lifted a glass to his friends. "I can't believe you pulled this off. I had no idea."

Nash mock-polished his nails on his arm. "Next

Cantwell endeavor: wedding planners."

Gideon almost choked on his champagne. "You know what, I can see you in that role. Of course, the next one you plan will be yours. You're the last one."

Nash hid behind his glass. "Don't bet money on it."

Isaac glanced down at the wedding band that now lay next to his engagement ring. He never would have been able to pull off something this nice. And he'd been unbelievably touched by the venue Delilah had chosen for them to exchange vows in. The reception hall was beautiful. Wedding guests had been enjoying the art gallery as well as the abundance of food. His eyes went back to Delilah. He wouldn't mind finding a hidden corner somewhere.

He didn't think he'd ever forget the sight of Delilah as she stood before him. She was stunning. The silvery dress shimmered in the sunlight. Her delicate hands held purple roses. Her red hair hung down her back and shoulders in luxurious waves. She'd kept her makeup light, and her lavender eyes held tears as she came toward him and agreed to be his wife.

It was Gideon's low swearing that pulled Isaac's attention away from Delilah.

Nash turned to where the men were looking. "I did not invite him."

Isaac swore. "No doubt he bribed someone to get in. The question is why. I'll take care of this."

Isaac stormed over to where his father stood with his mother. His father looked like he usually did. He wore a stodgy brown suit and tie. His mother wore a dress that was once lovely but now looked worn. Her eyes were pleading with him. When he stood before them, she gave him a peck on the cheek.

Isaac tried not to be swayed, but felt his anger soften. His mother, despite how he wished otherwise, could still find the soft spot in his heart that he had for her. "Should I even ask how you got in?"

Theodore Brandt straightened his shoulders and spine. "You should be ashamed. We had to hear about this wedding from our friends. You couldn't be bothered to tell us?"

Isaac kept his voice low. "I didn't imagine you would care or bother to attend. As Delilah pointed out, you couldn't be bothered when I was in the hospital. Nor did I expect you to."

Theodore's smile was all teeth. "We would have been humiliated. It's bad enough we missed the ceremony. Your mother will have to make excuses to our friends."

Isaac's voice held a tone of derision. "You could simply tell the truth. But I don't think you know what that is."

Theodore's false smile faded. "Dance with your mother. And then we'll have a friendly chat with your wife. We'll stay for cake and leave."

Isaac gave his father a mock bow and held his hand out to his mother. "Care to dance?"

Millicent gripped her son's hand as he led her to the dance floor. "Your bride is lovely. And this reception is beautiful. Your friend Nash's doing?"

Isaac's eyes widened in surprise. "I wasn't sure you even knew his name. But yes, this was partially his doing."

Millicent turned sad eyes up to her son. "Your father

likes to throw the Camhion name around on occasion. He finds your friendship with Nash beneficial. You look handsome. But then you always do."

Isaac held back what he wanted to say to her. She had been looking at his scars and damaged eye as she'd said it. "I always favored you."

Though not true, it made her smile. She reluctantly let him go when the song ended. She turned to look behind her. "Your father is coming. And your bride is glaring at you."

Isaac turned to see Delilah staring his way. And yes, perhaps glaring. He took his mother's elbow and didn't wait for his father. "You remember Delilah."

Lilah held out a hand to his mother. Her teeth were clenched when she spoke. "Lovely that you could attend."

Millicent only nodded when her husband came to stand beside her.

Isaac waved a hand at the quartet as they started to make their way over. It warmed him that they wanted to come to his rescue, but he didn't want to embarrass Delilah. She looked ready to toss them out. And he didn't need Trenton to make a scene, as he was likely to do.

They managed to have a civilized conversation. His mother had asked him about his books. His father inquired when he was going to get tenure. Isaac answered politely, though his answers were short. He could have kissed Delilah when she told his mother how lovely she looked, and his mother had blushed. She was the reason the conversation stayed on an even keel.

But he could see the strain in her eyes. Dinner was being

served. He tagged Nash to find a table for his parents. Nash not-so-gracefully complied.

Lilah leaned against him and whispered in his ear. "How long do they plan to stay?"

Isaac kissed her neck as he spoke. "Until after the cake."

"Mmm. Let's get dinner over with and cut that cake. We can sneak out after, too."

Isaac brushed his lips against her hair. "A woman after my own heart."

Nash had outdone himself with the lavish meal. It was his gift to the couple. As they were fixing a plate, Nash commented that he had adamantly refused to eat a boring, rubbery, and unimaginative wedding meal at his best friend's wedding.

Lilah took a bite of her food. Her eyes closed. "I don't know what this is, but it's heavenly."

Isaac opted not to tell her. "Everyone else seems to be enjoying it, too. I believe Trenton and Ginny paid for the open bar. But I think I'll stick to the champagne."

Lilah lifted her glass to him for a small toast. "So, Isaac, was your wedding everything you imagined it would be?"

Isaac chuckled as he tapped his glass to hers. "I think I'm supposed to be asking you that question. But no."

Lilah leaned over after taking a sip and kissed then bit his lip. "What did I tell you about learning to lie?"

His thumb rubbed her bottom lip. "It's so much more than I imagined."

She discreetly licked the spot she'd bit. "Mmm. That's better."

Isaac's voice was a growl when he found his words.

"Let's eat cake."

There were good-natured jokes about the haste with which the couple was rushing the reception, but Isaac ignored it. He was delighted with the blush on Delilah's cheeks. They engaged in the traditional sharing of the cake slices, and he enjoyed kissing the frosting from her lips. Cheers went up, and the cake was passed.

They ate their cake and the music started back up. Lilah stood and held her hand out to Isaac. "One last dance, Dr. Brandt?"

Isaac rose, his eyes heating. "Just one, Mrs. Brandt."

He gathered her into his arms as other couples joined them. Nash winked at him, Gideon nodded, and Trenton gave him a thumbs-up.

The last strains of the music faded. He was releasing Delilah when a loud shot filled the room and people started screaming. Isaac yanked Delilah behind him as he tried to see what was going on.

Gideon grabbed Nash and Trenton and shoved them at Isaac. "Keep him here."

Isaac watched in shock as Gideon pulled a gun out from under his jacket. Isaac shoved his way between Trenton and Nash, but the men wouldn't let him go any further. They created a wall in front of Delilah as they held his arms, who was leaning over his shoulder trying to see.

Isaac cursed and somehow managed to dislodge himself from between his friends. "Keep her here."

He heard Delilah yelling at him, her voice filled with fear, but he blocked her out. He rushed to where Gideon was yelling directions at guests in shock.

Gideon looked up from where he stood. "Go to your mother."

Isaac barely registered his father lying on the ground, Caleb Jones standing with his hands in the air, a pistol dangling from his forefinger, and his mother pale as she stood frozen in place.

Gideon took the gun from Jones, yanking the man's arms behind his back and cuffing them. He was reading Jones his Miranda rights as Isaac dropped at his father's side, yanking off his jacket to staunch the blood. He was barely aware of Delilah, who gave him a thorough once-over before going to his mother's side as Trenton called 911.

Nash, ever the consummate host, was gently pushing guests toward the other side of the room. His parents came to help. Ginny and Penny came to Lilah's side as she comforted Isaac's mother. Priscilla, with the help of Rob, came to stand by her daughter.

Jones watched the older man on the floor. "I only wounded him. He'll live. Though he'll wish he hadn't."

Isaac saw red. He jumped up and punched Jones square in the jaw. The man fell back several steps but managed to stay on his feet.

"What the hell do you think you're doing? You come into my wedding, upset my wife, scare my mother half to death, and shoot my father?"

Jones's eyes went back to Theodore. "Your father is a traitor."

Gideon held Isaac back. "You have an audience. We'll take him downtown and we'll figure this out. Officers will be here to take statements, but Jones surrendered, so they'll escort him out and take witness statements."

The next few hours were a nightmare. Guests who hadn't seen the shooting were ushered out. Those who did were questioned about what they saw. Nash dealt with the museum's director and staff to clear away the reception. Trenton drove Isaac's mother to the police station after Gideon took Jones into official custody and took him to the station.

Lilah stayed by Isaac's side. "Station?"

Isaac glanced down at his now wife. He was torn. He certainly didn't want to spend his wedding night at the police station. But he also wanted answers. After Jones's declaration that his father was a traitor, he had invoked his right to remain silent.

Lilah made the decision for him. She gave her mother a quick hug, then turned back to her husband. "Come on, let's go. Neither of us will be able to relax enough to enjoy our wedding night until you find out why this happened."

Chapter Fourteen

The station was still bustling. It was only nine o'clock, and the night was just starting for the officers assigned to the Saturday night shift.

Gideon came out to greet them. "Your father is stable and is now officially in federal custody. Guess who showed up?"

Isaac watched an older man, his hair now steel gray and a paunch over his once trim waist. "Monroe."

Monroe held his hand out to Isaac. "It's good to see you, despite the circumstances."

Isaac reluctantly shook the man's hand. "I can't say the same."

Monroe's dark eyes turned to Lilah. "Congratulations on your wedding. You've got yourself a fine husband."

Lilah ignored the hand he held out. "Want to explain to my husband why one of your ex-employees shot my father-in-law at my wedding?"

Monroe dropped his hand. He turned to Gideon. "We need a private room."

Gideon nodded and led them to an interview room. He closed the door behind them and stood between them and the door. "Spill it."

Monroe took a seat. "It's going to be a long night. Jones has been trying to get me to investigate your father for the past couple of months, not too long after Avery's arrest. Avery told some story about being blackmailed into betraying her country. Said there was a diplomat who found out she was stealing money from the government. So he forced her to sell the secrets she knew, and the diplomat wanted a cut. As she tells it, he blackmailed her into selling the secrets and turning over the money. She claims our military men who were killed along with several civilians were a result of the blackmail and the secrets she sold. Funny thing, your father is telling the same story, but in his version, Avery was blackmailing him. That as a diplomat he had contacts she wanted, and she threatened to expose him unless he did what she said."

Isaac took a seat at the opposite side of the table. "Expose him for what?"

"Fraud. He admits he was bribing people in other countries while in his official capacity. He said she found out through some mutual investment partners. Your father had a lot of cash tied up in overseas investments, not all of them legal, and many of which you could consider a conflict of interest as a representative of the U.S. government."

Isaac rubbed his brow. "So because you refused to investigate my father, even though Avery was telling stories of his involvement in her treasonous activities, Jones came and shot him at my wedding? And you didn't think I needed to know this?"

Monroe gave a non-answer. "You're no longer a civil servant at the Pentagon. It was need-to-know."

Gideon folded his arms across his chest. "And therefore Isaac had no need to know. You knew Jones would do this, didn't you?"

Monroe turned to Gideon. "Caleb Jones has been on a

mission to punish his brother's murderer and anyone who had any involvement in the conspiracy to sell government secrets. I found out Jones had sought Isaac out, and that our fine officers at the MPD were involved in trying to capture Avery. I knew it was only a matter of time before Jones figured out who Avery's partner was. He was always convinced she had one. Someone in your department has kept the investigation open, and that was Jones's window in."

Gideon took a menacing step forward. "There was a threat in D.C., and I wasn't going to let a traitor to the U.S. government murder Isaac. Unlike you."

Monroe just shrugged. "As they say, just business. I got wind Jones was tracking Dr. Brandt. The elder one. I just spoke with Jones, and he admitted he had heard about the wedding through some gossip at Georgetown. He made sure that Isaac's father heard about it. Then it was a matter of waiting. According to Jones, he watched Theodore go in, he mingled with the guests, and waited until Theodore was getting ready to leave to make his move. That way, he was far away from the guests. If it's any consolation, he said he had no plans to kill your father. But shooting him in a public venue was guaranteed to get the local police involved and force my hand. Your father will end up in the same prison as Avery."

Gideon visibly reined in his temper. "What window?"

"You. You found Avery's partner; the one who helped Avery try to kill Isaac. Jones used his contacts inside the police department and found the link between Dr. Brandt and Avery."

Gideon cursed. "Ramona."

Monroe nodded. "During your investigation, you're going to find that Ramona was the go-between for Avery and Theodore. Jones made the connection and made sure Theodore Brandt would come to the same end as Avery."

Isaac stood when Monroe did. "Anything else you've been keeping from me? Should I be on the lookout for someone to show up during my honeymoon?"

Monroe hid a smile. "Your father's arrest officially closes this matter. You can go about your business."

Gideon moved away from the door. "And my shooter?"

Monroe shrugged. "Book him for what you will. I won't be arresting him. But otherwise, he's on his own. Choices are dangerous things, and Jones chose poorly."

The trio watched Monroe leave.

Isaac pulled Lilah to his side. "Let's get out of here."

Lilah stopped and pointed at Gideon. Her voice was indignant. "Why did you have a gun at my wedding?"

Gideon glanced at Isaac before turning back to Lilah. "I had a bad feeling."

Lilah stepped away from Isaac and hugged Gideon. "Thank you. I think."

Gideon kissed her cheek and shook Isaac's hand. "Congratulations. Now go home."

* * *

Isaac led Lilah from the station. He stopped short when he spotted his mother by his car. "Mom? What are you doing here?"

Her hands were clenched in front of her, her eyes tired and filled with remorse. "There are federal officers raiding our home. I knew this day would come."

Isaac stopped his approach. "You knew what he had done?"

"I knew enough. Your father was never as smart as you. And he never had your integrity. Most everything your father had was the result of theft, blackmail, or threats. He wasn't afraid to use his diplomatic position to get what he wanted. I know our home is in foreclosure, and he has more debt than he can pay. But he's been even more stressed these past months. I guess we now know why."

Lilah spoke when Isaac didn't. "But you never turned him in. What if Jones had gone after Isaac instead?"

Tears dripped down her cheeks. "Theodore knew someone tried to kill Isaac. I overheard him talking on the phone. I was horrified that my son had been run off the road and that someone tried to kill him. It made me ill to know Theodore knew about it. He was talking to a woman who had helped. The same young woman he was having an affair with. Roberta or something."

Isaac found his voice. "Ramona."

Millicent nodded. "That's right. Ramona was also having an affair with some woman named Avery. Then I overheard him talking to someone else, and they were going to pin your murder on Ramona."

"So he was conspiring with Avery. Are you going to tell the police what you know?" Isaac demanded.

Millicent wiped her tears. "I wanted to see you first. I've nowhere to go. We have no money; the feds will no doubt seize what's left of our property, and your father is going to go to prison."

Isaac had no sympathy. "Prison if he's lucky."

Lilah stepped forward, laying a hand on Isaac's forearm. "You can stay at my apartment. I don't need it, and my mother and I haven't gotten around to emptying it out. No one is living there, and you'll have a place to live until we figure all this out."

* * *

Isaac tugged off his bow tie. "It was nice of you to let my mom stay at your apartment."

Lilah came and helped him unbutton his shirt. "She's your mom."

Isaac kissed her. "That's one of the things I love about you. Your compassion was one of the first things that made me fall in love with you. That and your eyes."

Lilah's hands went to the waistband of his pants. "Not my lush body?"

Isaac's hands untied her dress. He watched it slide off her body and pool at her feet. "That, too."

Lilah shook her hair back. "I love you, Isaac."

Isaac kicked off the rest of his clothes. He picked Lilah up and put her on the bed. His hands went to the edges of her purple lace underwear. "I can't believe this is all you were wearing under that dress. Thank goodness I didn't know. I'd have never made it past the ceremony."

Lilah giggled at that. Then she moaned when his fingers stroked her through the lace. "I've been imagining you removing them all night."

Isaac obliged. They teased and tormented each other until they couldn't take any more.

Lilah wrapped her legs around his waist. "Now, Isaac."

He went to grab a condom out of the nightstand.

She put a hand over his. "I think we should name our first child Violet if it's a girl. I haven't figured out how to incorporate Nash's, Trenton's, and Gideon's names into one name if it's a boy, though. I'm still thinking on it. But you're a genius, so I'm sure you can come up with something."

Isaac dropped the box where he'd grabbed it. "Let's see, Gidtrentnash."

Lilah laughed until her stomach hurt. "So much for being a genius."

Isaac kissed her and joined their bodies. "I'm sure I'll come up with something. But right now, genius or not, I want you."

Afterward, Lilah laid her hand over Isaac's heart and snuggled up against him. His hands toyed with her hair until he fell asleep. As he lightly snored, she peered at her belly. Perhaps not this time, but someday soon, they'd grow their family. And she thought she might be a little bit of a genius herself; she had, after all, picked Isaac for her own.

And then...

Nash lay in his bed staring at the ceiling. It was late, but he couldn't sleep. That was the norm for him. He turned toward the nightstand when his phone beeped. He laughed a little at the silly meme about vegan vampires. He dialed the number.

A woman's smoky voice came over the line. "Good evening, Ignatius."

Nash propped a pillow behind his head and relaxed. "Never going to let that go, are you, Freya?"

A muffled giggle over the phone was his reward for being a good sport. "I told you; I like it. Very dignified and old-fashioned. And you did say it was your grandfather's name."

Nash's muscles relaxed a little more. "Yes, but we called him by his middle name, Cormac, because he hated the name too."

She made a humming sound. "How was your day? I've been reading the press releases. Cantwell makes its official debut in a few months."

Nash closed his eyes and yawned. "A whirlwind for sure. We're ready for the release, but I'm anxious and excited to have it over with. Gideon is grumbling about having to take off work to make the publicity rounds. Trenton is threatening to buy a hot pink suit. Isaac is, well, Isaac."

Freya's smoky laugh came over the line. "I have only met Gideon, but I have heard enough about Trenton to know the threat could be real."

They chatted for a little while longer about her day at the crime lab. Nash yawned again. And he started to end the conversation as he often did. "So, what are you wearing?"

Freya had teased him about late-night phone calls and warned him he better not degenerate into lewd prank calls. As usual, Freya's words were soft as the hour grew late.

"Lab coat. Good night, Nash. Sleep well."

He set the phone aside when she hung up. He yawned again. He enjoyed their late-night calls. Other than his sister, Gideon's sister Iris, and his best friends' wives, he didn't have much in the way of female friends. He was never without female companionship if he wanted it. But he couldn't talk to them the way he did Freya. They certainly never listened to him as intently as she did, nor did they remember the things he had said. She did.

It had started with a text to thank him for sending her dinner. He'd done it on impulse when she'd helped the quartet locate the file on Avery Whitlock. He had done it again after she had found Avery's partner. After that, they had texted back and forth a little here and there. He hadn't heard from her for a while when she had sent him a silly meme. It had been accompanied by a message that said she hoped it cheered him up. She told him she had heard about Isaac's dad being shot during Isaac's wedding reception. He supposed it didn't take a genius like Isaac to know he was not in the best of moods in the aftermath, though he was surprised she would know how much it had upset him. In the aftermath of the shooting, all he could think was that it could have been Isaac. And after the shock of the shooting was over, it triggered memories of watching his grandfather shot all those years ago.

Surprisingly, he had found the meme humorous, and he found it touching that she cared enough to send the silly message and inquire how he was doing. Had it been anyone else, he'd likely have been rude, and she'd never have texted him again. Then the pattern continued as it had before. But then texting became occasional phone calls. Occasional phone calls became more frequent.

But despite their conversations, despite all she had done for his friends, he was reluctant to suggest they meet in person. Inevitably things would change. It sounded arrogant, but he was Nash Camhion. He was the sole male heir to a fortune. Women fawned at his feet. Women would blindly follow him wherever he went just to get the attention that constantly followed him.

There were always rumors and speculations about who he was dating, if he would get married, and when he would bring the next generation of Camhions into the world. He let them wonder. His sister might run the company, but when it came to social obligations and being the face of the family, he was the one people knew. He figured he owed his grandfather the courtesy of fulfilling his family duty. And it was his way of protecting his sister from his world.

He did wonder about Freya. He knew she was in her early thirties, knew she was smart, and that she spent most of her hours working. He tried to picture what she might look like, but the only thing he could see in his mind when he thought of her was Gideon's painting. It was fanciful, perhaps. Despite everything in his life, he did have a romantic streak. And Penny was convinced whoever the woman in the painting was, she was the woman destined for him. He wasn't sure why he associated the painting with Freya, but he did.

But if he brought Freya into his world, the gossip and sensationalized version of his life would follow her. And as dramatic as it sounded, she was from a different world than him. And the raw truth was, he didn't want to get married, and he didn't want to bring the next generation of Camhions into the world. Yet there was something about Freya that drew him in; that had him picking up the phone night after night and talking to her until sleep came. She brought peace and comfort into the darkness.

Tired now and feeling sleep would come, he rolled onto his stomach, bunched up his pillow, pulled the covers over his bare shoulders, and fell into a dreamless sleep.

The Quartet has been so much fun to write. Admittedly, Isaac was the hardest. What motivates a man like him? Who would love him like no other woman could? If you read my "From The Author" section in the previous two books, you'll remember the characters are based on characters in a video game. Isaac is based on the character that brought reason to the group. And the character could cook. He loses his vision trying to help his friends. I didn't take Isaac's vision, but I felt that going through what he did made him stronger and yet vulnerable. I think it softened Lilah's feelings toward him in a way nothing else could have.

Isaac didn't have a sordid past. When someone sets out to kill him, there is no question in his mind who that someone was. So in his story, there isn't a mystery as to who is after him. That was a departure for me. I rarely know who did it when I set out on my writing journey.

About the series: The Cantwell Quartet is centered around four men: the prince, the protector, the peacemaker, and the comedian. Not sure that is how the game writers thought of them, but that's how I do. The four men fight side by side to save the kingdom, and ultimately, the world. Each has flaws. Each has secrets and pain. And each of them does what's right. My kind of heroes!

I hesitate to name the game for two reasons. One, the books are not based on the storylines in the game, so I don't want to disappoint fans who think they're getting fan fiction, or a modern-day book version of the game. The books are my stories with my interpretation of who these men could be in modern day. And two, it's more fun to keep you guessing. But if you guess right, I'll tell you.

Also, if you enjoyed this book, or any of my other titles, please consider leaving a rating at your favorite retailer, Goodreads, and/or Bookbub. And if you have the time, a text review would be lovely. Indie authors rely on readers like you to tell others how much you enjoy their books.

Happy reading,

<u>Books by Elizabeth Castle</u>

Single Titles:
   Going Home
   This Kind Of Love
   Chasing Hope
   The Babe & The Librarian (novella)

The Heart's Way Series:
   For Now and Always
   Ask Me To
   Say You Love Me
   Forever Love

Bennett Family Series:
   This Time Love
   A Bride For David
(novella)

All Of Me Series:
   All Of My Days
   All Of My Nights

Cantwell Quartet Series:
   Falling Slowly
   Unraveled
   Hidden Away
   Entangled

Contemporary "Retro" Romance Series:
   Loving Jordan

Visit <u>elizabeth-castle.com</u> for newsletter sign up and up-to-date releases.